WHAT VOODOO DO YOU DO?

MATURE MAGIC

BOOK 2

SAM CHEEVER

ELECTRIC PROSE PUBLICATIONS

ABOUT ROME

Crafting worlds is crazy good fun. Authors love to make stuff up. Sometimes locations that are created for books seem like real places, even though they're not. That's actually good, because it means the author has done her job well. My fictional town of Rome, Indiana is not based on a real place. I've created a location that lives in my mind—one that fits the stories I wanted to tell. Hopefully you have enjoyed the picturesque town of Rome with all its paranormal challenges. I'm thankful for the opportunity to share this fictional town and its inhabitants with you.

xo

Sam Cheever

PRAISE FOR SAM CHEEVER

"You have that essential Je ne sais quoi that it takes to tell a story so mesmerizing you cannot stop reading once started. You are not telling stories to your readers...you are taking them with you on your adventures so that the experience can be shared by all as it happens and not simply replayed like a memory on the page of a diary! You are indeed gifted and it is my pleasure to read your books!"

Valerie Irwin

~

I'm discovering that glossing over that whole "epicenter of a magical vortex" thing when I took this Lares job was a mistake. Looking back, that now seems like important information.

Whoever said midlife was a time for reflection and relaxation clearly wasn't an ancient guardian deity. I'd just started to think I was getting a handle on this whole Lares thing, and then the earth decided to open up into a giant, fiery hole of evil nastiness.

Talk about your hot flashes!

Add in a deadly new ally, a magical weapon I'm pretty sure I'll never get the hang of, and being forced to play "Where's the Voodoo Queen" while trying to deal with everything else...well...let's just say that crepey skin is probably the least of my worries.

STAY IN TOUCH

Sam doesn't give away a lot of books. But she values her readers and, to show it, she's gifting you a copy of a fun book just for signing up for her newsletter!

SIGN UP HERE!
https://samcheever.com/newsletter/

A LARES SHALL HEROIC BE

When evil's core begins to rise, and devil's gaze on man resides, the Lares' spirit rules the day, if evil cannot earth hold sway, though love and loss be fairest friends, the guardian's tears will guide their ends.

A call to save the weak from harm,
A plea to sound the first alarm,
A rupture in the fetid soil,
A magic much like rancid oil,
The weak succumb to powerful fates,
The vessels for an oily hate,
A good man falls, a guardian weeps,
When virtue dares and evil sleeps,
With dangerous allies at her side,
Let failure pierce a guardian's pride,
Seen through an ally's jaundiced eyes,
The Lares must her peers apprise,
When malevolent forces spread their wings,
A deadly soup of horrendous things,
A guardian's light must burn and blaze,

To forge a path for brighter days,
Or let the darkness rise and rule,
Relenting means she plays the fool,
At last the end is coming clear,
The guardian's loss a thing to fear,
When golden days return at last,
The Lares must look to the past.

1

A CALL TO SAVE THE WEAK FROM HARM

Gong!

I jerked awake, the darkly melodic tones of the bell still reverberating through my mind. The sound was more than a warning. It was more than an invitation.

It was a summons.

On the heels of that realization, my cell phone rang. I shoved the covers off and swung my legs over the side of the bed, grabbing my phone. "Hello?"

Monty trotted past me and hit his doggy stairs, descending at a run and disappearing down the hall in the direction of the kitchen.

"Is this Aggy?" the voice on the phone asked.

"Yes. Who is this?" I didn't recognize the voice, but something about it rang a familiar note.

"Oh, thank heavens!" the woman said. Her voice was rusty as if she'd been pulled from sleep as she'd done to me. She coughed wetly as the force of her exclamation tore at her throat. When she spoke again, her voice broke beneath her words. "You need to save us. This is cataclysmic."

I stood and headed for the sweatshirt I'd thrown over a nearby chair. "I'm sorry. Who is this?"

"It's Molly. Molly Stanton. From Golden Years senior home. We need your help, Madam Lares. We're about to be overrun."

I hesitated, remembering Molly from my days of working at the senior facility. As I recalled, the eighty-something-year-old woman had been strange. Beyond strange. I suspected she had a touch of dementia. I glanced at the clock and grimaced. Three AM. "I can come in a couple of hours," I told the octogenarian. "Would that be okay?"

The tension in my shoulders relaxed as I realized the crisis I'd been expecting was probably just the creative imaginings of a woman with compromised faculties. I grabbed a hair clip off my bedside table and smoothed my straight black hair back, twisting it into a quick bun and clipping it to get it off my face.

Monty's claws tap, tap, tapped up the hall. The sound of something dragging along the floor as he ran sent a chill through my system.

"No! You have to come *now*. Please, Madam Lares."

I frowned at the title. Non-magical humans didn't call me that. They didn't know about my newly-minted guardianship. When I'd worked at Golden Years, I hadn't had any magic. At least none that I'd known about. And Molly had seemed just as human as I was. Which, looking back, just might have proved the point I was missing. If I could become an ancient Roman deity in the space of weeks, there was no reason to assume Molly couldn't become something...more...too.

Monty trotted into the room with his leash clutched in his mouth, bounced up to me, and dropped the leash on my feet. He barked emphatically, his fringe of a tail whipping enthusiastically behind him.

The leash thing was new but not surprising, given that everyone and everything in my life seemed to be embracing a magical core. The bat in my belfry (not a metaphor, I actually had a bat in my belfry) was magical. My adopted mom and sister were magical. I had a magical raven that sometimes showed up out of nowhere. My gardener was a gnome. The sexy man candy in my life had wings. The contractor working on my renovations was a warrior fairy. And the ancient brass bell in my belfry (again, not a metaphor.) was enchanted.

I fully expected my single-serving coffee maker to someday sprout hands and make the coffee for me.

If only I could get my oven to make pumpkin muffins...

A sharp, terrified scream came through the phone line, followed by a roaring sound that rolled over the screaming and swallowed it whole.

"Molly?" I yelled into the resulting silence. "Molly? Are you still there?"

Down by my feet, Monty whined. He shoved the leash with his long, black and tan nose. "Woof!"

I paced my room, my nerves atwitch with the feeling that something cataclysmic had just happened. Without warning, the foundation of my pretty little church slash home slash business shuddered beneath a concussion so powerful it nearly threw me to the ground.

Monty lunged in my direction, dancing on his back legs in a terrified plea to be held. I scooped him up and ran toward the front door. Flinging it open, I ran out onto the small front porch and searched the darkness for anything that would explain the explosion.

In the distance, beyond the picturesque town of Rome,

Indiana, the sky was lit with a pale red glow. Beneath the glow, the horizon burned gold and orange and smoke lifted to the slate-gray sky.

Fire! I grabbed my cell again and dialed 9-1-1. The phone rang and rang, but nobody responded.

Something was wrong. Very wrong.

Shoving the phone into my pocket, I said, "Come on, little man. We need to go find out what's happening."

Golden Years Senior Home was an old facility. It had been in its current location since I was old enough to ride my bike into the country with my friends and head to the reservoir only a couple of miles away. Despite their age, the buildings had been well-maintained. The facility had gone through several owners over the decades of its existence, and each one had put his or her own personal brand on it.

A hodge-podge of styles and a mix of tastes, Golden Years was an ugly sucker, rising from the corn and soybean fields on either side of it like a boil on the verdant earth.

I climbed out of my car and eyed the building, not seeing any damage that would explain the explosions I'd heard. And felt.

The parking lot held only one car at that time of night... day...and the windows were mostly black. The door in the glass-fronted entranceway was locked, as expected, and a soft light inside showed no activity in the lobby.

Goochy Goochy Goo, Your Mom Needs you. Goochy Goochy Go, She Won't Take No!

Goochy Goochy Gum, You Know You Can't Run. Goochy Goochy Glee, You Know You Can't Flee.

"Curse, curse, swear!" Why did I leave her alone with my

phone? I hit the button to answer the call from Mavis. "Mom. You know it's the middle of the night, right?"

Mavis and her daughter Bev had been my family in every way that counted since I'd lost my birth mom to cancer when I was fifteen. My ex-husband was Mavis's son. Their family had lived next door to mine back then. Mavis had opened her heart and home to me from the day my mother died, treating me like a daughter, even as Bev treated me like a sister and best friend all wrapped up in one. Neither of them had ever wavered in their support or love.

But Mavis had recently formed an annoying habit of changing my ring tone to weird, mother-themed songs when I wasn't looking.

"Actually, *Aggy*, it's early morning." Mavis didn't sound like her usual, sunny self, but I wasn't surprised, given that it was three-thirty in the curse, curse, swear morning! "What's going on? I felt something," she demanded.

"You felt that explosion?"

"Something exploded?"

"You didn't feel it?"

"No. What exploded?"

"If you didn't feel it, why are you calling me?"

"Because I felt...something."

I clamped my lips together, scrubbing a hand over my face. Monty dragged his leash past me and trotted over to a nearby bush to pee. "I'm standing outside the Golden Years Senior Home right now," I told her. "Molly Stanton called and begged me to come out here because there was some kind of danger. Then I heard an explosion."

Mavis's voice shook slightly, and I heard the sound of keys jangling. "Don't move from that spot. I'll be there in five minutes."

I opened my mouth to tell her everything looked fine,

but was confronted by dead air. She was gone. Sighing, I walked over to the keypad on the wall and punched in the code to unlock it. Luckily, I'd recently resumed my regular visits to the home, bringing the ever-bubbly Monty along to enthrall and delight the residents. They'd given me the code so I could come and go as I pleased.

I stepped into the darkened building, listening to the soft whir of air moving through the ducts. As it had appeared from outside, the lobby was empty. That didn't surprise me since the night nurse stayed pretty close to the resident rooms in case there was an emergency. The place was only dimly lit via security lights over both exterior doors and a small lamp on the table next to the couch. I started toward the door into the resident wing. "Come on, little man," I told my dog. "Let's go find Molly."

Light flickered past the windows overlooking the courtyard, jolting me to a stop. Monty took off toward the light, barking a warning I couldn't ignore. Flames suddenly bathed the air beyond the doors. I turned and started running, hitting the bar on the glass door with momentum and diving out into the fiery night.

I expected to see burning buildings. Or, at the very least, a large fire in the enclosed courtyard. But what I saw was much stranger than that.

And infinitely more terrifying.

2

A PLEA TO SOUND THE FIRST ALARM

I managed to step on Monty's leash before he got away from me. Slipping my hand through the loop, I held on as he did everything he could to escape my grip and get to the nightmare unfolding in front of me.

The world roared and burned as if I were standing beneath an army of attacking dragons. But there was no smoke. There was only fire, which sat upon the grass without burning and slipped along the ground as if testing its taste and texture.

The noise seemed to be coming from the center of the space, where a small decorative well wavered behind the type of aura caused by waves of excessive heat over an asphalt road. The tiny bucket hanging from a metal rod over the well waved violently as if an unseen hand continually shoved at it. The heated air spun with the colors of fire around the decoration, the light source appearing to be somewhere underneath the well.

A familiar figure stood on the far side of the yard decoration. Molly's head was thrown back, her soft white hair dancing around her small head and her frail arms stretched as if in supplication.

I moved through the strange atmosphere of the courtyard, the heated air pushing back at me with every step I took. Eyeing Molly for signs of awareness, I noticed her eyes were closed and her lips were moving.

What in the curse, curse, swear was going on?

A burst of red and yellow light flared from the well and shot skyward, the sound like an explosion from a small cannon. The light hung suspended above my head, reflected off the glass of the dozens of windows overlooking the courtyard space. A shadowy shape moved through the light, its motions frantic and aggressive.

Monty yelped and ran back to me, pressing his trembling body against my legs.

As I stared into the strange illumination, a heated jet of air smacked into me, taking me to the ground, and a husky laugh, as deep and gritty as a sinkhole in the desert, boomed around me. Monty nervously licked my face. He wanted me off the ground.

Heeding his warning, I shoved to my feet, instinctively grabbing for the power coiling in my core. I held the energy at my fingertips, feeling its anxious bite on my skin. But I didn't throw it for fear I'd hurt Molly in the process of battling whatever had invaded the once-tranquil space.

"You have no influence here, Lares," the voice informed me.

I took a surprised step back before I could stop myself. The faceless, shadowy entity perched above me seemed to fold into itself, reaching for me with amorphous limbs that made the air crackle and spit.

Monty lunged at the shadow, snapping his jaws as if he could stop the voice by biting it.

Panicking, I let my magic dance around my hand as I tried to find the source of the disembodied voice. I felt the need to fight back but didn't have a target.

The laughter filled the space, pinging off the building and bouncing back to me even louder than before. "You have no influence here, Lares," it said again. A rotting meat smell rose up around me, the stench so strong it made my eyes water.

"You're repeating yourself," I yelled, stalling for time while I tried to pinpoint the source.

More laughter. The sound sliced through any bravery I'd managed to muster like a butcher's knife. Panic layered me in a cocoon that dulled my surroundings. Monty's frantic barking sounded far away, though I could feel his furry body pinging frantically against my legs. I fought the urge to turn and run. But my gaze was drawn back to Molly. I yelped in fear. The diminutive woman stood only three feet away, and her eyes were a solid black.

Monty snarled and lunged at the elderly woman, shocking me with his aggression. I shortened the leash, keeping him close to my legs. But when I looked into Molly's face, I saw what Monty no doubt had already seen.

Something that wasn't my friend was looking out at me through her eyes.

Molly's cotton-candy hair still blowing around her skull, her lips were curved into a smile that belonged on a long-dead corpse. She stood with her gnarled hands layered over her rounded belly, observing me as if I were a particularly fascinating bug.

"Molly?" I sent out a wave of energy and could barely feel her essence beneath whatever was riding her. "Molly, you need to fight this off."

A foul-smelling wind surged up from the ground and

wrapped around my legs, ripping them out from under me. Monty yelped and tugged the leash from my nerveless fingers. I crashed to the ground on my back. The force knocked the air from my lungs, ensuring that I couldn't scream when the invisible energy around my calves lifted me off the ground and slammed me into the brick wall of the building.

Agony flared quickly as my flesh hit the hard, biting surface, but I couldn't dwell on it because I was suddenly flying across the courtyard to smash against the opposite wall.

Immediately, I was flung into the sky, so high that I came even with the top of the shadowy illumination infesting the courtyard.

For just the briefest of seconds, I thought I saw a face in the shadows. Round black eyes and a bovine nose above the curve of scabby lips around deadly-looking fangs. Then I was flung downward again, seeing my death in those hate-filled eyes.

I gathered my energy and pushed against the power that had hold of me, using my own energy in an attempt to sever its control. I threw everything I had at the entity, watching with satisfaction as the illumination changed form, spun on the air, and then plunged downward into the decorative well.

I hung in the air for a heartbeat and then plummeted toward the ground.

Massive wings beat the air above my head. I barely had time to acknowledge the presence before strong arms snatched me from the sky. I screamed, arms flailing until I realized who had hold of me. Then I sagged with relief, allowing him to ease me to the ground.

I clung to Lungren Maker like he was a lifeboat on the

surface of a storm-tossed sea. My entire body shaking with fear and residual adrenaline, I clutched his shirt and buried my face in his delicious scent. "Oh my goddess," I murmured unintelligibly against him. "I thought I was a goner."

Gren's arms came around me and held me tight. "Just breathe, Aggy. Pull air into your lungs, and let it slowly out." His warm hand rubbed my back, inspiring delicious thoughts even while it soothed my jangled nerves. "Tell me what happened."

I lifted my head, looking into his fathomless dark brown eyes. "There was a summons. And then I got a call..." My words drifted away, and my eyes went wide. "Molly!"

We found her crumpled in a limp pile where I'd last seen her. Her tiny form looked so lifeless, I thought she was beyond our help.

But as Gren gently turned her over and I felt for a pulse, her bright blue eyes snapped open and she stared up at us, looking thoroughly confused. "Am I inside a romance novel?"

Gren and I shared a look. I was afraid the dementia that had a grip on her mind was in control.

But Molly laughed, winking at Gren. "He's a hottie. Introduce me, Aggy."

"Molly, this is Gren. He's my..." Our gazes caught and held across the prostrate woman. Heat painted my skin wherever his gaze touched it. "Um..."

Gren turned a smile on Molly. I wanted to tell him to tone it down a bit. The eighty-some-year-old woman could have a heart attack at the sight. "Aggy and I are the best of friends. Would you like to get off the ground?"

Molly's mouth was open, her gaze locked on his. "Ground?"

Gren chuckled, the sound sexy and seductive.

Molly and I both swallowed and blinked under its force. "Come on," I told the woman. "Let's get you up. How did you get out here, anyway?"

Molly allowed us to lift her gently to her feet. She frowned, her soft hair like a halo around her tiny, wizened face. "Out where?" I watched as she finally realized where she was. "Did you bring me out here?" she asked, looking alarmed.

"No," I told her, easing her onto a nearby bench. "Do you remember calling me?"

"I called you?"

I was pretty sure she hadn't been under the influence of that shadowy thing with the scabby lips when she called me. "Yes. You asked me to come because something was happening here."

Molly nodded, swiping a hand over her mouth. "Yes. I do remember that." She stared at her hands, the skin pecan brown and crepey with age. "But I can't remember why I called."

"There was some kind of explosion," I told her. "I rushed over and found the courtyard full of fire that didn't burn." I was looking at Gren, telling him even as I filled Molly in. "And wind that wasn't really wind." I shuddered. "Molly was standing over that little well over there, her arms outstretched. It looked like she was doing a spell or something."

Gren walked over to the harmless-looking wooden well and looked down into it, his stance going rigid. "Abby."

I touched Molly's shoulder. "Don't get up, okay? I don't know what that thing did to you. I don't want you to fall."

She nodded, her eyes locked on Gren. Or, more precisely, on his backside.

"Molly." My voice held a note of censure.

Molly didn't seem to care. She briefly tore her gaze away from Gren and winked at me. "Let an old woman dream, cher."

I rolled my lips to keep from grinning. "I'll be right back."

Gren didn't turn to me when I approached. Every line of his tall, muscular form was taut, his hands clenched at his sides. I knew it was bad before I stopped beside him and looked down.

The sides of the small, wooden well rolled and boiled as if something writhed beneath the cheap wood. The nearest side-wall bowed toward me as if the entire thing were made of stretchy fabric. I stepped back in alarm as the distinct shape of a clawed hand groped the spot where I'd been. "What is that?" I asked Gren.

He turned a haunted face to me. "I don't know. But whatever it is, it's just about as evil as anything I've ever felt, Aggy."

I had no problem believing that. The clawed apparition retreated and I stepped closer, peering down into the well. I gasped, one hand coming up to cover my mouth. "Oh my goddess!"

The space inside the yard ornament appeared infinite. Boiling with inky black magic, it was alive in the way nightmares lived. The movement of the magic drew me in, enthralling me before I even knew what it was trying to do. I stared into the shimmering roil of energy, watching as it fought its constraints and tried to bubble to the top of the limited space.

Like a pot of boiling pudding, it rose thickly toward the edge of the well, sending seeking threads toward the lip in an effort to lock on and pull itself out.

Every time it managed to clamp on, a shiny geyser of energy burst at its center, sending grave-scented air into our faces and ripping the questing magic back down.

"Something is keeping it from escaping," I told Gren.

He nodded. "It seems to be fighting itself."

"Weird," I said.

"Beyond weird," he agreed. "You should call the witches."

The witches... I blinked. "Curse!" Spinning on my heel, I hurried toward the door. "Mavis was coming to help. She's probably locked outside." As I rushed past Molly, I said. "Don't move."

She was still watching Gren as if he were a sizzling steak and she hadn't eaten in months. Her lazy grin was creepy, but in a lecherous older woman way, rather than a monster boiling in a well way. "No worries, cher. I ain't movin' from this spot."

Rolling my eyes, I yanked open the door into the lobby. As soon as I stepped inside, my phone started ringing, and there were a series of dings as several texts popped onto my screen.

I answered the call while hurrying toward the front door. "Mavis, I'm so sorry!" I shoved the door open and came face to face with my angry mom. "I have a good excuse for forgetting you. I promise!"

3

A RUPTURE IN THE FETID SOIL

"I've been standing out here for twenty minutes," Mavis complained, pushing past me into the lobby. "I thought you'd been eaten by demons or something."

I felt my hazel eyes go wide. "Demons? Why would you say that?" Was I the only one who hadn't expected a demonic presence and a Hellmouth in the courtyard?

She blew a raspberry. "It's just a figure of speech." Her expression turned sly. "But you do realize Rome is built on top of a vortex to Hades, right?"

At the horrified expression on my face, she laughed, her good nature returning. "Just teasing, honey. That's just an ugly rumor. There's no such thing."

I winced. "I wouldn't be too sure about that."

Mavis walked past me into the lobby. "Why didn't you answer my calls? Or my texts?"

I stared at the texts that had all arrived as soon as I'd come inside. "Something was apparently blocking them. Maybe the courtyard is a dead zone."

Mavis didn't look convinced, but she let it go. "Where is everybody?"

"I assume they're sleeping."

Her brows lifted. "Even Shadee?"

Shadee was the night nurse, a no-nonsense Amazonian with coal-black skin, a wild halo of curly black hair, and eyes that pierced your soul and ripped the truth from reluctant lips. She was also one of the kindest, most compassionate people I'd ever met. "That is strange, isn't it?" I agreed. "The explosion wasn't exactly quiet." The realization made me panic. "There must be something wrong with the residents."

The door to the courtyard opened, and Gren came inside, carrying a limp and unconscious Molly in his arms.

I panicked. "What happened? Is she okay?"

He laid her down on the couch. "I'm not sure. One minute she was ogling my backside, and the next her eyes were rolling up in her head. Then she collapsed."

Mavis bent over the unconscious woman. Once upon a time, a couple of decades earlier, Mavis had been a nurse. She quickly assessed my friend, a worried frown playing across her face. "This isn't purely physical, Aggy. There's the stench of black magic about her." She lifted her gaze to me. "Tell me what happened while I was cooling my heels outside."

Curse, swear, curse! She wasn't going to let that go anytime soon. I told her about finding Molly standing over the little well, the monster in the tower of light and shadow, and being used as the whacker in a magical game of whack-a-mole.

Her expression finally softened on that last part. "Are you okay, honey?"

"Yeah," I said. "It takes more than a shadowy demon to

dent *my* head." I'd been going for humor, but Gren and Mavis both winced. So, I tried again. "This Lares thing seems to have made me kind of invincible. But getting smacked into a building still hurts like a mother," I admitted.

Mavis patted my hand, looking down at Molly. "I'm not sure non-magic medicine will help her, but she needs to go to the hospital. After that, we'll look at alternatives."

"Alternatives?" Gren asked.

Mavis nodded. "We might need to fight black magic with black magic."

My eyes went wide. "You mean, like voodoo?"

The door behind me smacked shut with a loud clang. "Voodoo ain't black magic, cher," a booming voice said. "It's a religion. I'll give ya dat da rituals to deities can be misused by some."

Shadee strolled toward us, the whites of her eyes bright in the dim light. The woman was six feet tall and built like a swimmer, with broad shoulders, narrow hips, and the longest legs I'd ever seen. She was dressed in blue hospital scrubs, but even in the soft, slouchy clothes, she still looked stunning.

The night nurse looked about as spooked as I'd ever seen her. "But, in dis case, you're right." She stopped next to the couch and looked down at Molly, her smooth brow furrowing. "Dis energy dark. The devil done got inside dat poor creature," she said in her deep, husky voice. "It gone take jus' 'bout everyting we got to drag his sorry behind out o' dere."

"You think she's possessed?" I asked.

"I'm not sure about dat." Shadee jerked her head toward the courtyard. "What happened out dere?" she asked.

"You didn't see it?" Mavis asked.

"Na. I bin takin' care o' all dem old folks in dere. Whatever blasted through dat barrier sent a shrill tone into da air and knocked dem all off dey feet. I got bloody heads, broken noses, and I'm worried about a few hips. Da ambulance is comin', and I don't have a clue what ta tell 'em happened here."

Knowing we were about to be interrupted, I quickly relayed the story again, keeping to the pertinent facts and leaving out some of the detail about my too-close association with the walls and ground.

"Dat vortex still in da well?"

"Yes," Gren said. "It's trying to escape its bounds."

She frowned. "I'll see if I can slow it down some."

"Slow it down?" I said. "We need to stop it."

Shadee threw me a look, her dark brows arching. "Yeah, Lares, we do. But if dat da vortex out dere, it gone take more'n jus' me ta stop it. We lookin' at a whole lot o' heartbreak if we don't get dat ting shut down. Ya feel me?"

I did feel her. I felt a lot of things. And none of it was good.

"Is there any point in taking her to the hospital?" Mavis asked, nodding toward Molly. "Can they help her at all?"

"Dat sister los' to da magic. Ain't nothin' no human doc can do ta help." She blew air between her lips and put her hands on her narrow hips. Sirens speared the unnatural quiet beyond the doors. Shadee's head snapped up at the sound. "We need ta block dat vortex from dem humans."

Mavis nodded. "I can do an obfuscation spell. And I'll see if I can slow it down while I'm at it."

"Tanks, cher," Shadee said, glancing at me. "You can help me in here? We need ta do triage."

"Of course."

"I'll go keep an eye on Mavis," Gren said softly, squeezing my elbow.

I gave him a grateful smile. "Give me a call on our special line if you need me."

It will be my pleasure, Gren said in my mind.

Despite the dire situation we found ourselves in, the sound of his sexy voice in my head warmed me right down to my toes. Shoving the warm fuzzies away, I fell into step behind Shadee. I struggled to keep up with her as she strode quickly through the door to the patient rooms, her long strides making two of mine.

As soon as we entered the residence part of the building, I noticed all the open doors, which seemed odd. What was even odder were all the bodies laid out in the social area of the space. Elderly people were draped over the floor with pillows under their heads and blankets covering them. I saw the knots and wounds on their pale, papery skin immediately. The bruises and blood stood out against their paleness like beacons. Most were awake, their rheumy gazes following us as we approached, but three of them in the first row were unconscious. A woman and two men. The woman's face was covered in blood from a hairline wound. The arm of the man next to her was draped carefully across his chest, the stark white of a bone piercing the skin. The other man had one leg that jutted at an odd angle.

Shadee looked at me. "I gave dem sometin' for da pain. Dey old bones don't hold up well to trauma."

Tears filled my eyes. I wondered if I could do anything with my power as Lares to help them.

As if she read my thought, Shadee shook her head. "Let the human docs help dese folks. It's da natural ting. It always best ta go wit natural whenever you can."

I nodded. "What do you want me to do?"

"Da hospital could only send two ambulances. We need ta triage dese people so da EMTs can just come in, fill dey gurneys, and get dem out o' here. Da sooner dey leave, da sooner dey can come back for more."

"Got it."

Shadee motioned me toward the front when someone knocked. "Let 'em in, cher."

We triaged, soothed, gave water, and added pillows for the next two hours while the ambulances worked their way through the injured. By the time the last patient left the building, the sun was peeking over the horizon, and I felt as if I'd already put in a full day's work.

Which I had.

"Was everybody affected?" Mavis asked, looking a little peaked when she finally came inside.

Shadee shook her head. "Dere's Mrs. Wolde and Old Mr. Pintwallen. He be fine 'cause he's deaf as a shoe." She chuckled. "Drives me batty, he does, refusin' ta wear dem dang hearing aids. Always with da, 'what now?' 'what you say, honey?' I never thought I'd be happy when he couldn't hear sometin'." Her formidable brows lowered. "Mrs. Wolde is jus' a little mouse. She's as shy as dey come and don't speak much ta strangers. Somehow she came out o' dis widout a scratch." Shadee shook her head. "Da two o' dem gonna be lonely widout da rest."

"Some of the residents should come back soon, right?" I offered. "Not all of them were badly hurt."

Shadee nodded. "Dey gotta check dey bones and heads. Make sure dey ain't nothin' goin' on dat'll hurt 'em in da long term."

"How do we close up that vortex out there?"

Shadee's gaze slid to the glass separating us from the courtyard. "I wish I knew, cher."

I yawned widely, exhaustion suddenly finding me. "Okay. I'm going to go swim in a vat of coffee, then call my council together and see if we can come up with a plan."

"I'll hit da books and call some of my friends," Shadee promised. "We'll figure dis out, Madam Lares."

Nodding, I headed toward the door. "You know how to get in touch?"

"I do."

Mavis and I didn't speak until we got outside. The long, perfect form lounging against my car straightened and walked toward us as we stopped beside Mavis's shiny new SUV. Gren cocked his head, his dark brown eyes narrowing. "You look exhausted."

I didn't deny it. "There's a lot of coffee in my near future."

Mavis patted my arm. "I'll call Bev and have her bring donuts."

I pulled her into a hug. "Thanks for your help, mom."

She held me tight, squeezing harder than a woman in her sixties should have been able to. But, I'd recently learned that Mavis wasn't human. She and her daughter, my sister of the heart, were witches. And I was learning that witches were a unique and powerful bunch. When she pulled away, her smile was sad. "You know this is going to get real ugly, real fast, right?"

I frowned, wanting to ask for more details, but knowing it didn't make sense to go into it without the rest of my council there. "Not really. I don't know anything about demons. But I'm expecting that you all are going to enlighten me."

With a nod and a tired smile at Gren, she climbed into her cute SUV and drove out of the lot.

I turned to my sexy savior. "Well, here we go again," I

said, a smile curving my lips. I might be dumber than a shirt made of hair, but there was a tiny part of me that was excited for what was coming. Things had been strangely quiet in Rome for nearly a month. And while the hiatus had given me time to work on the church remodel, I'd missed the thrill of adventure and nearly daily brushes with death my seating had offered.

Yeah, I know. Dumb as hair.

Before that seating, which was kind of the training and testing phases of becoming a Lares all wrapped up in one cluster curse of an event, I hadn't known I had a magical legacy. Or even that magic existed.

Barely a month later, I was fighting demons.

Curse, curse, swear!

"Yes, here we go again," Gren agreed.

"You want a ride home?" I wasn't exactly sure where "home" was for Gren. He usually just kind of walked into or out of the shadows around the church.

"Unless you want to fly on Air Lungren?" He raised his brows, waggling them suggestively.

I laughed, shaking my head. "Right now, I'm almost too tired to drive. Unless you've got a saddle for your back, I doubt I could stay aboard."

He stepped closer, and the air darkened behind him, the impression of enormous, dark wings lifting above his head. He touched my chin, lifting it so he could look me in the eyes. "I would never let you fall, Aggy."

Too late.

I was pretty sure I'd already fallen into a puddle of goo at his feet. "Uh..." I slammed my lips shut and swallowed hard. "Ah..."

Gren lowered his head, and I forgot to breathe. His soft

lips found my skin, burning a brand on one of my superheated cheeks. "I'll see you at home."

Then, with a swish of the wings that seemed to be nothing more than shadow, he was gone.

"Dang!" I said, laughing at myself. "I should have taken that flight. Maybe there would have been a layover somewhere spicy and hot."

That thought kept me warm and awake during the short drive home.

4

A MAGIC THAT'S LIKE RANCID OIL

"Tell me about this vortex," I instructed my team. We were seated in the former sanctuary, which I'd transformed into a beautiful living space with clusters of comfortable seating and tons of plants in front of the stunning focus area of floor-to-ceiling arched windows. The brightly-hued rugs Bev had helped me pick out pulled each seating area together and warmed the oak plank flooring, creating a vibrant visual experience that never failed to bring a smile to my face when I walked into the room.

The space was also a perfect spot for me to meet with the twelve members of my council. There was plenty of seating and room for all of us. Though Reverend Dodson, being a ghost, didn't really need seating, and the bat and the raven didn't need furniture either if they ever both showed up at the same time, which hadn't happened yet.

Lately, Wraith, the black cat that had decided she wanted to be part of our little party, joined the meetings too, much to Monty's delight. He loved having a friend to play with. Though, in fairness, the *play* was kind of one-sided.

Monty did zoomies around the sleek feline, bounced and barked, and generally made a nuisance of himself, and Wraith bathed herself, ignoring him.

The black cat had just turned up one night, draped over a tombstone in the church's small graveyard. I'd begun feeding her not too long after that because…well…I couldn't seem to help myself. And she'd wandered into the kitchen through Monty's new dog door not too long after that.

Wraith had been keeping watch over the place since that day, really more of a bodyguard than a pet. But I was pretty sure she was warming up to us.

Sort of.

Maybe?

It's really hard to tell with a cat.

Lungren stood in front of the window alcove, staring out at the grounds. I watched him standing there, wondering what he was thinking about so hard. Also, my gaze might have drifted, once or twice, to one of his better features. (I was referring to his broad, muscular back, potty brain.)

"The vortex has been there through millennia," Ferral, my advocate, told me. His tone, which was clipped and snotty as usual, made the statement sound like scolding for my ignorance. "It's been inactive for decades."

I turned to look into his too-handsome face, focusing my hazel gaze on his dark silver one. As usual, Ferral's shoulder-length wavy blond hair was unbound, his muscular form covered in a perfectly tailored suit. The current version was black, over a starched white button-down shirt that was open at his muscular throat. He seemed to favor a dark gray suit generally but wasn't afraid to mix it up with black or navy on occasion.

He was a real party animal like that.

"What could have happened to activate it?" Bev asked, frowning.

Reverend Dodson shrugged his shoulders, which looked nearly corporeal since he was standing in a shadowed corner. "The last time this happened, a coven of witches had been trying to call a demon through blood magic." He slid his kind brown gaze to me. "Does anyone at Golden Years Senior Home know how to perform that type of magic?"

"I'm not sure. I know of two women living at the senior home who came from Louisiana. I guess there could be more. I'm pretty sure that one of them has voodoo in her background. I'm not sure about Molly."

"Molly's the one who's been possessed?" Bev asked.

"Shadee, the night nurse, wasn't sure about that," I said. "Shadee's mother was a voodoo queen in New Orleans. I assume she knows about dark magic too. It would be hard to grow up around voodoo without picking some things up about its darker side."

"How well do you know this night nurse?" Trish asked. Sitting in her favorite chair, she'd tucked a sock-covered foot under her leg while tapping the toe of her other foot on the rug.

As usual, Trish was dressed in a well-worn denim shirt over a tee-shirt and heavy work jeans. She'd removed her work belt and dusty boots when I'd summoned her from the room where she was in the process of constructing my candle shop.

The pretty contractor had baby-soft blonde hair and vivid green eyes that crinkled in the corners. When she wasn't working as my contractor, she was an ancient fairy warrior of the Unseelie branch. She was also part of the same coven Mavis and Bev belonged to. Apparently, her magic was compatible with theirs. I suspected the "coven" was mostly an excuse to drink wine and eat. But I could be wrong.

"Not well. I know Molly better. Why?"

"I was just wondering if she was comfortable with her magic."

I shook my head to show I didn't understand what she was asking me.

"Does she embrace her heritage? Or seem embarrassed by it?" Bev clarified. She tugged off an elastic ponytail holder and resmoothed her straight blonde hair into a short pony at the back of her head. With a few quick, practiced twists, she secured the shoulder-length bob and sat forward, elbows on knees.

"I don't know. But I'll find out." I sighed. "We need to close that vortex before it affects others like Molly."

"Tell us about the vortex," Luke asked. The wolf shifter had dark brown hair and golden-brown eyes. His square jaw always sported sexy stubble. I realized I'd never asked him what he did for a living, but I suspected it was something to do with construction. He'd done some work with Trish in the past.

Taking a deep breath, I expelled it in a rush. I sat back on the couch and tucked my feet underneath me. "You know those cheap little wooden wells they sell in garden centers for people to stick in their yards?"

Their heads bobbed in unison.

"It's in one of those."

Silence met my admission, along with a few stunned looks.

"Seriously?" Trish asked.

"Seriously," I agreed. "Weird, huh?" Then I remembered Monty's frantic contribution to the battle and amended my description. "At least, it used to be in the well. I'm afraid

Monty shoved the well over. It's probably all over the ground now."

Mavis shook her head. "It doesn't work that way, Aggy. That stupid well bobbed right back up after a few minutes. The vortex was still inside."

"For now," a deep voice said from the front of the room. We all turned to look at Gren, whose intoxicating face had turned my way. "That vortex is not only active, but it's dynamic."

"What does that mean?" I asked.

"It means it's growing," Niele said. The gnome's thick features folded into an unhappy look. He ran short, wide fingers through his frizzy silver hair and pursed his lips. "That's really bad news," he said.

I was happy to see he was wearing the moss undies Bev had made him. I'd discovered the hard way when moving into the church that, although gnomes were excellent gardeners, they liked to do their gardening in the buff. Unfortunately, Niele had no patience for most fabrics and had resisted covering his stick and berries until my brilliant sister created the moss underwear for him.

"You've felt something?" Ferral asked the gnome.

"I have," Niele agreed. "The layers of the earth are shifting, making way for something. I was nearly lost to the changes this morning. I assume that's the vortex pushing its way upward."

"Wait," I held up a hand to stop them. "We saw the vortex. It's already on the surface."

Ferral shook his head. "No. You saw a questing branch. Nothing more."

I opened my mouth to ask, but Trish spoke before I could. "An active vortex has hundreds of, for lack of a better word, feelers. It sends them out on a continual basis, looking for a path to the surface."

"Once it reaches the surface," Bev added, "this particular vortex will become a Hellmouth, providing direct access to the creatures of the demonic plane."

I swallowed hard. "What creates the path?" I fought a shudder as ice crawled along my spine.

"Magic," Gren said. "The darkest kind of magic." His gaze found mine, tiny lines creasing the smooth skin between his eyes. "Somebody in that place used blood magic, Aggy. And we can't close the vortex or save your friend until we find out who it was and stop them. Hopefully, we're not already too late."

THE FRONT DOOR opened and slammed closed. Already keyed up after Gren's dire announcement, I twitched violently at the sound. I glanced through the wide doorway to the foyer and saw a familiar but unexpected face. A straight bob of midnight hair brushed the teen's narrow shoulders, and a slender gold nose ring pierced her small nose. Wanda's dark brown eyes stared back at me, their contours exaggerated with thick lines of black eyeliner.

As usual, the teen was dressed all in black. Midnight-hued skinny jeans covered her too-slender legs like leggings beneath an oversized black tee-shirt with a silver pentacle on the front.

She looked at me in surprise and I blinked back.

It was only noon. Much earlier than she usually arrived at my house. A fact that was made starker by the fact that Wanda couldn't control her visits to the church. The teen was the victim of a groundhog day type spell, which was placed on her by witches, judging from Wanda's recounting of the event.

She'd once told me the spell seemed to occasionally suffer from glitches, and I guessed her early arrival might be one of those. "Just in time," I told her, motioning her into the room. "We were discussing our latest crisis."

The teen slunk reluctantly into the room, dropping into a chair set apart from the others and looking suitably morose for her goth-like presentation. When everyone looked at her, she made herself small and tried to become one with the tea roses in the upholstery. "Dudes!"

Mavis grinned. Bev laughed. The men looked confused.

"We're just surprised to see you so early in the day," I told her.

Wanda generally popped in at dinner time and left within a couple of hours. Her early appearance made me wonder if Bev and Mavis's attempts to remove the spell tying her to the repetitive behavior were having an effect.

The girl shrugged. "Whatever."

We stared at her a beat longer, waiting for her to finish the sentence. We were disappointed in that expectation.

"Okay, then," I said. "We have an open vortex at the senior home outside of Rome. Do you have anything to contribute to the conversation on how to shut it down?" I really didn't expect her to, but the kid surprised me on a regular basis.

Wanda sat up straighter, a look I'd seen before sliding over the bored expression she'd been nurturing. "Vortex?" She frowned.

I watched her expressive face turn thoughtful as she considered my question. I didn't know nearly enough about Wanda since she didn't like to talk about herself or her situation. It had been like pulling teeth just to get the story of how she was spelled out of her. But I was starting to recognize two things. First, she was wicked smart. And second, she had magic. It wasn't a type of magic I'd ever heard of before, but it was very useful magic. She knew stuff. Random, strange stuff. About the magical world.

"The last vortex opening in this area was around nineteen-thirty-seven. It ate the entire downtown, and a mile in every direction before the current Lares managed to shut it down."

My throat threatened to seize up at her words. An experienced Lares had nearly been unable to stop it? I was toast. "Yikes!" I said, panic flaring.

She ignored me, seemingly lost in her thoughts. "But the vortex was the least of it."

I felt my eyes go wide.

"Demons flooded from the Hellmouth and found hosts among the townspeople. Before the Lares and his council realized what was happening, the hosts had killed many of the remaining townspeople."

My head dropped into my hands, which felt cold as ice against my fevered brow. *Curse, curse, swear, swear!*

"What opened it?" Mavis asked, her gaze sliding worriedly toward me. I wasn't sure if she was concerned that I was about to roll into the fetal position and drool on myself or because of Wanda's news.

Either way lay calamity.

"A local coven let itself be swayed into playing with blood magic by a powerful warlock who was the brother of one of the coven sisters. They thought he was just going to summon a low-level demon and then send it back. An exercise in stretching their wings, magically speaking. But he had bigger plans. He wanted the vortex open. And, once it was open, he killed the coven sisters who'd helped him open it."

Bev swore softly. "With only a few exceptions, a vortex that's been magically opened can only be closed by those who opened it. And even that's not a guarantee."

Wanda nodded. "His actions ensured the vortex would stay open for a long time."

I thought of the summons that had alerted me in the wee hours of the morning. "Why wasn't the Lares warned what was happening?"

Wanda slid me a look I couldn't interpret. "He was warned that *something* was happening. But one of his council members was killed within the hour and, either the Lares believed that was what the warning pertained to, or he just got sidetracked by grief. The history is unclear on that point."

Both her non-Wanda-like delivery of the information, with nary a "dude" in the bunch, and her mention of "history" reinforced my perception that Wanda's magic was tied somehow to magical records.

I thought about her words, a feeling of unease sliding through me. It just wasn't jiving for me. I'd had a few nebulous warnings since taking my place as Lares of Rome, Indiana. But the important ones sent me directly to the problem. Or maybe I was just getting better at reading the warnings. I wasn't sure, and that bothered me.

"How did the Lares eventually close the vortex?" Ferral asked.

Leave it to the grumpy advocate to get right to the root of the issue.

Wanda threw me a look that made me uncomfortable. It was a look I wasn't used to seeing on her young face. Dread, possibly mixed with unhappiness.

"What is it?" Gren asked.

Wanda fidgeted with a string on her tee, her gaze avoiding mine.

"Wanda?" I nudged.

She expelled a gust of air. "There has to be another way."

"What?" Niele asked, shifting on his chair.

She finally slid her gaze to me, and the impact of that look made me rear back. My heart was pounding so hard and fast in my chest, I was afraid I might pass out. "Just tell me," I said. My voice was barely above a whisper.

Licking her lips, Wanda finally said. "He threw himself into the vortex and sealed it from the inside with his magic."

5

THE WEAK SUCCUMB TO POWERFUL FATES

Deep inside my dreams, I transformed the ringing phone into the gong of the bell in my magical belfry. I turned the notes I heard into cartoon flowers that sifted away from the bell on air currents created by singing birds.

I know, crazy, right? And I hadn't even had any wine the night before to explain my strange dreams. Mumbling at the bell, I told it to be quiet, and rolled over, pulling my pillow with me on a weary sigh.

Gong!

Where the cartoon flowers hadn't even come close to waking me, the real thing ripped me from sleep and yanked me upright on the bed. Blinking dazedly, I looked around for Monty, but he wasn't in bed with me.

I scrubbed a hand over my face and yawned. Nails clicked down the hall. My little fuzz-butt came through the door with his leash in his mouth again. I narrowed my eyes at him. "What gives?"

He barked happily, his tail wagging with canine enthusiasm.

Climbing wearily out of bed, I shuffled toward the bathroom to do my thing. "I think *you* should become Lares. You're better at this than me."

He barked again, dropping the leash and dancing around it.

"I know. I know. Just give me a minute to p…" My cell phone rang again, the sound like bullets hitting my brain in the morning silence. I narrowed my gaze on Monty. "Did you do that?" He didn't answer me. Of course he didn't. He only cocked his cute head and gave me a doggy grin.

I washed my hands and hurried back into my room to grab the phone. As I answered, my gaze slid over the plastic tarp hanging from the ceiling on one side of the room and the fine layer of dust coating everything. I sighed. Trish had been making great progress turning the three rooms on the north side of my house into a master bedroom and bath and my future candle shop.

But everything would grind to a halt until we solved the pesky vortex problem.

Even as I had the thought, a sense of despair swept over me. What if I had to throw myself into the vortex to stop it from growing? My pretty little church-house would never be finished. Was that what had happened to the last owner? The one who'd remodeled the kitchen and nothing else? I shook off the dire thought and answered the call.

"Morning, Shadee," I said into the phone. "I'm leaving now."

"Bring your staff," she said, her voice sounding husky as if she'd just been yanked from sleep as I had.

The call disconnected. I looked at the phone with a frown. My staff? I didn't have any staff. I had a council. Was that who she'd meant?

Scratching sounds brought my attention around to

Monty. He was scrabbling beneath my closet door, his fuzzy butt in the air.

"I'm not going to change, buddy," I told him, grabbing his leash. "Come on." I'd taken to sleeping in yoga pants and loose t-shirts since taking up the Lares gig. There were just too many middle-of-the-night emergencies with the job. I'd gone in my PJs once and never wanted to do it again.

Gren was never going to let me forget the dachshund-covered PJs or the hot-pink fuzzy slippers I'd worn to save a little girl and her family from a deranged family member.

Speaking of dachshunds, my very own little food terrorist was digging more frantically beneath the closet door, whining unhappily.

"Monty, come on, or I'll have to leave you here."

He dove toward the door and tried biting the wood. I could already see deep scoring in the soft pine. "Hey!"

Then it hit me. *The staff*. Shadee had been talking about the pretty stick I'd gotten when I became Lares. Under encouragement from my dad, who I'd recently learned was also a Lares, I'd tried to play with it once. That would be the last time. I'd exploded a tree in my front yard, sending it toward the clouds like a leafy rocket. After that, I decided to use the stick as a prop only. A prop I never intended to use. "Oh, swear no," I said.

I walked over and picked up my dog. "Come on. If you got the summons too, the fates must want you there."

He slid a bright brown gaze back toward the closet where I'd hidden the stick after the tree incident, whining softly.

"Nope. Not doing it. Not until I have time to figure out how to use it without blowing everything up."

I deliberately shoved the traitorous thought that I'd had

a few weeks of relative quiet to practice. If only I'd been woman enough to risk blowing up another tree.

Nope.

I tucked Monty into my car and closed the door, heading around to the driver's side. A shape detached itself from the shadows near the house and I yelped, a hand flying up to send a golden wash of energy flaring outward.

The shadow was no longer there.

Instead, my magic hit a large bush near the candle shop door, blowing a cloud of dark green leaves into the air.

The light from my magic illuminated the hard lines of a stern face with dark silver eyes that were snapping with pique. "What have I told you about letting your emotions rule your actions?" The snotty advocate asked.

I pulled air into my lungs and released it in a frustrated gush, before glaring back at Ferral. "What have I told you about sneaking up on me?"

To my surprise, he grinned, which only made him look more striking. I shook off the notion and let my magic ease away. "What are you doing skulking around my house?"

"With the vortex opening nearby, we decided you needed someone to stay close. Just in case."

My lips twitched. "You drew the short straw?"

"Short straw?" He frowned. "Why are you talking nonsense?"

His snottiness sucked the smile right off my face. "Never mind. You might as well come with me to the senior home. Shadee called. Something's happened."

MONTY LED the way to the entrance of Golden Years, which, to my surprise, was unlocked. The interior glass door was also unlocked, and the lobby was again empty. I peered around the usually pristine place, frowning. Something felt off about it. Even if Shadee hadn't called me, I'd have known that something was wrong.

"What is it?" Ferral asked. He moved up next to me, his silver gaze sliding around the lobby.

"I don't know. Something feels..." I rubbed my hands over my arms, feeling gooseflesh beneath my palms.

"Like rancid oil coating your skin?" he asked, grimacing.

"Yeah. It's nothing I can put my finger on. But the place feels spoiled somehow."

He slid a finger over a nearby table, showing me the oily soot he'd picked up. "Hell smut."

I raised my brows. "Are we talking dirty pictures here?"

His brows drew in.

I shook my head. "Never mind. I'm guessing that's some kind of dirt?"

Ferral nodded. "Smut is a fungus. It gives off a dust-like substance that clogs everything."

"And why is the lobby covered in Hell smut?"

His gaze slid to the glass doors leading to the courtyard, where some kind of illumination danced across the glass. It wasn't fire. But something was flickering beyond the door. "The Underworld is full of the stuff. It covers everything and makes it hard to breathe." He nodded toward the courtyard. "I can feel the vortex from here. It's like being wrapped in razor wire covered in acid."

I grimaced. "Thanks for that mental picture."

Without responding, Ferral turned on his heel and strode toward the outer glass door. I started to follow and stopped, a sense of unease prickling beneath my skin. Glancing toward the door separating the resident rooms from the lobby, I murmured, "I should go get Shadee." She'd called me in. She deserved to know what was going on. Besides, she might be able to help us stop it.

"Madam Lares?" prompted a deep, arrogant voice.

I turned to Ferral. "I need to go get the night nurse who called me."

"Was she the only one here?" he asked.

"Yes. Why?"

Ferral's expression softened briefly. It happened so quickly I would have missed it if I hadn't been focused on him. "There's no need to get her," he said, his gaze sliding toward where I knew the vortex to be. "She's out here."

The way he said it sent ice crystals flowing through my veins. I hurried toward him, steeling myself for something I suspected would stick with me for a very long time.

I slid through the door, and Ferral let it close.

If I'd been blindfolded, I would have still known that something evil permeated the space. I felt its stain against my skin, its foul stench biting at my nostrils.

It was the reek of brimstone and death, overlaid with the putrid odor of hopelessness.

The vortex had burst the bounds of the tiny well. It had spread into a rough-edged circle that stretched toward the building's walls on three sides. The open side had spread across the courtyard, its churning edge a mere fifteen feet away from where Ferral and I stood.

But it was what hung above the vortex that caused my stomach to twist in fear. I gasped as I realized what it was.

A large form hung in mid-air five feet above the maelstrom. The figure was covered in a dark robe, its hood covering the person's head and falling in tattered wisps from large hands and long, strong legs. The face was shrouded by the hood. The body disguised within the loose, ratty robe. But I recognized the small piece of blood-red cloth wrapped around an assortment of herbs and small bones and tied with beads. The gris-gris had hung around Shadee's neck for as long as I'd known her. As far as I knew, Shadee wore the amulet all the time, rarely taking it off. She'd once told me a powerful gris-gris woman in New Orleans had made the talisman for her and that it had kept her safe for three decades.

The bits of bone and herbs didn't seem to be protecting her anymore.

Hot tears slid down my cheeks and, without thinking, I started forward, magic snapping at my fingertips. I would get her away from that monstrous Hellpit or die trying.

Ferral grabbed my arm and stopped me. "You can't help her now. The best thing we can do is kill the vortex. If she's still alive, hopefully, the witches can save her then."

I knew deep in my heart he was right. But seeing her that way, my memories showing me her bright eyes and wide smile, it just about killed me not to do anything. "We have to help her."

Ferral didn't respond. A fact which told me more than anything how dire the woman's situation was.

I stared at the obsidian surface of the maelstrom. It boiled with oily menace. Something moved beneath the surface. A constant switch and swirl that gave the impression something was going to burst free at any moment. My mind told me to run. But my sense of duty kept my feet stationary on the sooty ground.

As Ferral had predicted, Hell smut covered every available surface, painting the brick walls in clogging soot and flattening the once green grass beneath its weight. The concrete sidewalks that circled the small courtyard and led to the pavilion in the center were covered in the stuff too.

Their once-bright surface had turned a dull leaden gray beneath the smut.

The stuff filled the air, painting the windows until they were opaque and making it hard to breathe.

Monty bumped against my leg and I looked down. He was staring at the space above the vortex, his usually bright gaze dark with fear. A low, constant growl rumbled in his throat.

I held tight to his leash, not wanting him to get too close to the Hellpit. Even as we stood there, I sensed the edges expanding a fraction of an inch. Left to its own devices, the thing would easily consume the entire building within the week.

A deep, overwhelming sense of urgency flooded me.

I had to stop it.

6

THE VESSELS FOR AN OILY HATE

I looked at the advocate. "Any idea how to stop this thing?"

Ferral's frown deepened at my question. "No. I just wish the Historian's information had been more helpful."

"Historian?"

"Yes," he said, turning to me. "The girl. Clearly, she is a magical chronicler. Though, the spell clouding her aura is a bit perplexing."

"That's a groundhog day curse. I'll tell you about it after we stop this thing. Maybe you'll have some ideas how we can rid her of it."

He nodded. "Obviously, we aren't going to fling you into the Hellmouth as she suggested."

I thought he was having a little fun with me, but when I looked at his face, he appeared perfectly serious. "I'm glad to hear that."

He nodded, completely missing my sarcasm. "The dilemma is that the vortex isn't vulnerable on its exterior. We can pelt magic at it all day long from out here, and it will just go about its business." He covered his mouth with a hand, brows lowering in thought.

"I think I can put a pretty big hole in it with my magic. Wouldn't that kill it?" Despite my determination not to use the staff, I was thinking its super-sized, highly-uncontrollable energy beam could probably pierce the maelstrom pretty deeply.

"No. The vulnerable area is too deep below the surface. You'd need to get closer to do any harm." His gaze slid to Shadee, and he squinted. After a moment, he swore softly.

"What?" I followed his line of sight.

Ferral sighed. "Use your sight to see."

He'd said something similar to me once before when I'd missed some magical tethers and nearly killed Wanda as a result. At the time, I'd somehow managed to pull the invisible strings of power into view...metaphorically making my eyes into a pair of magical binoculars...but I had no idea how I'd done it. I chewed my lip, unsure I'd be able to do it again. Taking his cue, I squinted my eyes.

Nothing.

Shadee seemingly floated above the abyss, face down and spread-eagled, with no discernable strings keeping her in the air.

With a sigh, Ferral reached over and gently pushed my head forward. I resisted, "Hey!"

"You're looking too high," he said in a voice that was filled with disgust. Apparently, my lack of magical training was a constant source of frustration for him.

Poor baby.

I adjusted my view downward and squinted again.

Nothing.

The soft fluttering of wings behind us had me whipping

around, energy biting my fingertips as I prepared to blast the bat hovering above my head into next week.

Vibrant yellow eyes stared down at me, the batlike wings stroking the air. The creature made a series of squeaking sounds as if trying to tell me something.

I shook my head. “It’s no use,” I told it. “I don’t speak bat.”

Look again, a familiar voice said inside my head.

I stared at the bat. “I *have* been looking.”

The bat hovered on the air, its scary yellow eyes locked on me.

Sighing, I turned back around. Staring at the space above Shadee, I still saw nothing. So, I slid my gaze downward.

And gasped.

A thousand micro-thin strands of energy rose out of the muck of the abyss and pierced Shadee’s aura. My first thought was that the vortex was holding her there. But then a worse thought hit me. “Is it…?” I swallowed a sudden lump in my throat. “Is that thing feeding on her?”

Ferral grimaced and crossed his arms over a broad chest. That was all the answer I needed.

A soft wash of air coated the side of my face as the bat fluttered between us. *Yes.*

My knees softened. “Oh. Goddess. No.” In that moment, I understood why the previous Lares had flung himself into the abyss to kill it. The thing had probably taken a vulnerable victim to feed upon, and he hadn’t known of any other way to kill it.

“There has to be a way…”

Ferral’s gaze narrowed on me. “Have you been practicing with your staff as I requested?”

I almost laughed at his choice of words. Ferral didn’t

request anything. He demanded. Which, due to a serious character flaw in yours truly, was guaranteed to make me dig in my heels. "A little."

Make that one time. Blowing up the tree had scared the fudge right out of me, and I'd marched back into the house and stowed that sucker in the far back corner of the closet. Out of sight was out of mind.

Mostly.

His squinty gaze told me he didn't believe it. "You must contact your father."

I blinked in surprise. "Why?"

"He can train you in the use of it. Your staff is meant to be like your right hand. It's key to doing your job. You must learn how to wield it."

Pushing aside the memory of Shadee's last words to me...*Bring your staff*...I shook my head. "This is no time for me to get bogged down by training. We need to fix this, or Shadee's toast."

Clearly exasperated with me, Ferral made a little sound that was suspiciously like a growl. "What does a hard piece of bread have to do with that voodoo queen?"

I just shook my head. I didn't have time to teach the advocate English either. "Trust me on this. Learning how to use that stick is going to take me a while. There will be a lot of chaos and exploding of nature in the interim. I need to keep my focus on the problem at hand."

Besides, I couldn't help thinking, I didn't need training to blow holes in things. I'd already mastered that.

He stared at me a moment as if trying to see past my skull into my brain. Then he shuddered. Maybe he'd found his way to the part in my mind where I stored all my grooming secrets.

That was enough to make anyone shudder.

Goochy Goochy Goo, Your Mom Needs you. Goochy Goochy Go, She Won't Take No!

Goochy Goochy Gum...

I stabbed a finger on the screen to stop any more of Mavis's poor taste in jokes from staining the smut-filled air. "Hey, Mom. Ferral and I are at Golden Years again. The vortex is bigger. Lots bigger. And..." I swallowed hard. "It's got Shadee."

There was a beat of silence, and then Mavis's familiar voice came through the line. "Aggy! You need to hurry. There's a demon in town. And it's going to kill somebody."

I FELT my eyes bugging out as we entered Rome. The usually quaint town looked like a tornado had gone through, flinging cars, concrete flower boxes, and anything else unlucky enough to cross its path into the street. Uprooted trees dotted the small park in the center of town, and several store windows had been shattered.

The streets were mostly empty, but a few people huddled behind closed doors and a green SUV, sitting alone in the center of the street and surrounded by dented and steaming cars, had a wide-eyed couple in the front seat.

I parked the car at the curb beneath an old-growth tree a few blocks away from the edge of town, and Ferral and I climbed out. I went back and forth on leaving Monty in the car before finally deciding to bring him with. It seemed the demon had a thing about flinging cars around.

There was no way I was leaving my little man helpless and alone inside my car.

Without a word, Ferral disappeared in a burst of silver energy and then reappeared, his sleek, gray moon hound form oozing residual energy. He cast a silver-hued gaze up at me. *I'll sniff the demon out. Try to stay hidden until I find it.*

I nodded, one icy hand desperately clutching Monty's leash.

Watching the sleek, two hundred pound hound melt into the shadows and make his way up the street, I couldn't help wondering if the existence of the demon had something to do with the maelstrom at Golden Years.

It was a big coincidence if it didn't.

I wasn't a fan of coincidences.

Monty's head jerked up, and his bright gaze locked onto something across the street. I followed the line of his sight and saw nothing except a rumpled, dirty old man who looked like he slept on the streets. It wasn't the first time I'd seen a street person in Rome. It happened more than made me comfortable. I didn't like to think of someone in my protectorate sleeping outside, without food or facilities. It broke my heart, and I wanted to fix it.

Without giving too much thought to whether it was a good idea, I started toward the man. He wasn't safe on the street right at that moment. In fact, it was a miracle he hadn't been killed already.

Monty bounced along beside me, his tail straight out behind him, snapping the air. In canine body language, his tail told me he was borderline hostile.

He didn't like the cut of the old man's jib.

I'd proceed with caution. The man's greasy head lifted as we approached. I smiled. "Hi. Are you doing all right?"

The homeless guy's thin lips pursed and shifted as if he were chewing something. His too-slender face was heavily lined, and greasy strands of gray-brown hair fell to his shoulders in lank strands.

He was crouched against the gray brick wall of Rome's

only bank, *Rome Savings and Loan.* I noticed his filthy hand was wrapped around a chipped mug that was missing its handle. The bank's logo was visible on the side of the mug, and my gaze slid to the dumpster in the nearby alley.

Had he pulled the broken mug out of that dumpster? What else had he pulled out of there? I grimaced at the thought.

"Are you hungry? Do you need some money?"

Handing out cash wasn't really my thing. I'd been burned before when I'd given cash to people who lived on the street and then watched them carry the cash to the liquor store rather than the local grocery for food. But everything on the street had closed up. If I wanted to help him, cash was all there was.

A sour stench wafted from the man. He continued to work his mouth, the deep creases in the skin around it telling me the facial tick had probably been with him for a while.

I shifted closer. If I could get him talking, maybe he'd relax and I could help him get to safety. "Did you see what did that?" I asked him, nodding toward the uprooted trees and battered vehicles. As I glanced toward the street, my gaze caught on the couple in the forest green SUV.

The woman's eyes looked like they might pop right out of her head. She fixed me with a terrified look and gave her head a single, rigid shake.

I frowned. What was that all about?

The sound of cloth shifting against cloth brought my head back around. Sunlight climbed out from behind a distant tree line, the light catching in the man's copper-colored eyes and giving off a strange aura that was there one second and gone the next.

Beside me, Monty growled a soft warning.

Wings fluttered high above my head. I glanced up as the sun was temporarily eclipsed by the striking figure spreading a thirty-foot span of wings and then tucking them, diving directly toward me.

With the sun in my eyes, I thought, at first, I was being attacked by a demon. But Monty's staccato bursts of angry barking, interspersed with snarls that lifted the short hairs all over my body, brought my gaze back to the man in front of me.

He was no longer sitting on the sidewalk. His form, strangely, was tall and straight, his expression no longer tentative.

As I watched, the man lifted his arms away from his body and, with a leering smile toward the airborne creature diving our way, he sprouted enormous black wings that looked a lot like Gren's and turned to face me.

I sucked in a shocked gasp, backpedaling into the street and pulling a reluctant Monty with me.

Aggy, run! Gren's voice screamed inside my head.

But it was too late. The thing's gaze turned on me, vibrant red like fresh blood. With only the slightest tensing of his muscular form, he shot forward, slamming into me with a force that carried us across the street and smashed me into the stone and wood front of the *Pretty in Pink Boutique*.

I fought the muzziness clouding my thoughts as my body tried to absorb the damage from the impact. Claws dug into the flesh of my shoulders, sending breath-stealing jolts of agony through me as I struggled to shove the demon off my chest.

Its mouth opened and two rows of slimy yellow teeth, triangular and wickedly sharp, sprayed spittle that smelled like rotten eggs over my face and throat.

Without warning, the teeth lowered to my neck and speared my skin.

My screams swallowed any awareness of the world around me. My hands clawed at the thing in a panicked frenzy. I was dimly aware of Monty's little body whipping around my legs, snapping and snarling. The monster at my throat lifted its head, yanking its teeth from my flesh, and looked down at my dog, kicking out with a clawed bare foot and missing as Monty, at a speed that seemed impossible, dodged and lunged, biting and snarling. Amazingly, the filthy fabric covering the demon's muscular legs was torn and covered in blood from Monty's attack.

My little hero. My dog was taking it to the demon while I stood there and screamed like a worthless idiot.

Feeling ashamed, I jerked energy into my hands and slammed my palm into the creature's throat, sending it flying on a wash of golden energy.

Before it crashed into the buildings on the other side of the street, the thing was scooped out of the air by Gren.

A roar of outrage filled the empty street as they shot skyward, wings pounding as they flew straight toward the sun.

I pushed myself away from the wall, every muscle in my body screaming at me. Scooping Monty off the ground, I buried my face in his soft fur. "Thanks, buddy."

He whined and frantically licked my face, which was his way of telling me he was worried.

Madam Lares, are you okay? Ferral trotted up to me, his sleek canine form disheveled and covered in dirt.

Monty's tail wagged enthusiastically at the advocate's arrival.

"I'm fine." Looking toward the sky, I added, "Gren's

dealing with it now." The two forms were so small, I realized they had to be really high in the sky.

You're bleeding.

I bit back a snarky response. Something along the lines of, "Thanks for the update, Commander Obvious." Instead, I started across the street. The young couple was still in the car, their gazes focused straight ahead even as I approached. "What happened to you?" I asked Ferral.

"Just a bit of a scuffle. I dealt with it."

My hand on the car door, I eyed him for a beat. His haunting silver gaze locked on mine. There was nothing in his gaze that implied a desire to explain further. Apparently, he'd told me as much as he intended to on the subject.

Sighing, I yanked the car door open and looked inside. "Are you hurt?"

Neither of them looked at me. Neither spoke.

Beside me, Ferral tensed, his furry body pressing against my hip. *Aggy, I don't think...*

I wasn't destined to find out what he thought. With a snarl and a burst of surprising speed, the man behind the wheel turned and shot out of the car, clamping his teeth onto Ferral's throat before either of us could react.

7

A GOOD MAN FALLS, A GUARDIAN WEEPS

The moon hound yelped in surprised pain. I barely had time to decide what to do before the woman sprang off the driver's seat and hit me in a flying tackle. We smacked the hard asphalt and rolled, my hands flat on her shoulders and elbows locked, trying to keep her gnashing teeth away from my throat.

Deep inside, beneath the immutable need to survive that had me reaching for my magic, I realized the people who were attacking the advocate and me were victims. They'd been demonically possessed. They were different from the thing that Gren was fighting. As I struggled to keep the snapping woman away from my throat, despair rose up like bile in my throat. There was something in the woman's eyes...a residual horror...a frustrated kindness...that flashed a warning in my mind.

Ferral, they're possessed. Don't kill him.

Caught up in fighting for his life, he didn't respond. The possessed man was straddling him, fingers curved like claws and digging into Ferral's throat. The human's arms were covered in claw marks, and several bleeding holes perforated his throat. But his terrifying red eyes were alight with a fanatic's gleam. He didn't seem to feel any of the wounds.

Like a zombie.

I shuddered at the thought and slammed a foot down onto the asphalt, catching my assailant off guard and rolling us over before she could stop me. I lay on top of her, one arm shoved beneath her chin to keep her mouth away from my flesh.

"Aggy!" A familiar voice called out. "What can we do?"

Bev's long, slender legs appeared in my line of sight. I couldn't risk a glance up to her. "Do you know a spell to knock these two out?"

Another pair of legs, partially covered in khaki-colored capris, appeared next to Bev's. "Yes. They're possessed?"

The woman beneath me bucked hard and nearly managed to unseat me. I fought for control, managing to get her back underneath me. My arm slipped and she managed to clamp her mouth down hard on my wrist, her jaws strong enough to compress my bones as the skin ripped.

I bellowed in pain, nearly giving in to the desire to rip my arm away. Anything to stop the excruciating pain.

Monty flew into the mix, snarling and snapping at the woman's unprotected face. His teeth drew blood from several bites before he got hold of the skin at her throat and tried to shake her like she was a mouse.

Bev slapped the woman's head with an open palm that was infused with energy, and the glowing red color of her eyes dimmed, sifting away to show the human brown beneath. A beat later, her eyes rolled back in her head and she passed out.

"It won't last long," Bev said, crouching down beside me. "The demon is strong. Much stronger than their human will. It will fight its way through that spell in minutes."

"You need to get that taken care of, honey," Mavis said, taking my hand in a gentle grip. "Human bites are nasty. You don't want it to get infected."

I wondered how dangerous demon bites were. "Later," I said, pushing to my feet. "Right now, you two need to find a way to subdue them long enough that we can lock them up."

I became aware of snarling and snapping a few feet away. Ferral was still tumbling around with the man. Both of them were bleeding. "Can you knock him out too?" I asked Bev.

She smiled a little meanly. "Ferral? Gladly."

Despite myself, I grinned. "Don't tempt me."

I heard that, the cranky hound said in my head.

I snorted out a laugh.

Aggy!

My gaze shot toward the sky and the winged creature barreling toward the ground. *Gren! Are you okay?* Even as I asked, I realized he wasn't okay. He wasn't okay at all. He was falling way too fast, his wings fluttering around him as if they were shattered. His legs were bent at odd angles.

Monty whined, his tail tucked.

I'm sorry, Aggy. I couldn't... The voice in my head was husky, broken, threaded with pain. The words he'd spoken sifted into silence, and I realized he'd passed out.

I must have made a sound because everyone looked at me. "What is it, honey?" Mavis asked.

I watched Gren hurtle toward the ground, knowing he wouldn't survive the impact from that height. "I have to help him."

Ferral trotted over, his soft warmth pressing against my hip. *You must stop his fall, Madam Lares. You're nearly out of time.*

"I'm well aware of that!" I screamed, losing control of my temper. I threw up my hands and sent a wave of energy flying toward Gren, praying it wouldn't be too late. He passed the tops of the nearby trees, a mere twenty feet from the ground. It was a distance he would travel in the blink of an eye, the unforgiving ground awaiting him.

Inexplicably, a word in a language I didn't recognize fell from my lips. "*Cernerse*!"

Gren plunged downward, his big body limp, tangled mahogany hair covering his gorgeous face. My heart pounded in my throat as I watched, certain I'd been too late. Why hadn't I acted more quickly?

Behind me, Mavis gasped, followed by Bev's yelp of fear.

Ferral pushed closer but said nothing.

Gren's body was inches from the ground. Still, he fell. I fought to keep from closing my eyes. If he was going to die because I was too weak to save him, I wasn't going to look away.

If he died, it would be my fault.

With an abrupt jolt that made his entire body shudder, he yanked to a stop. I drew in a breath for the first time in moments, my knees softening beneath me. He'd stopped in time! Barely.

My protector and friend hung so close to the ground that it looked as if he'd landed.

A heartbeat later, with the soft sound of displaced air, he settled gently against the pavement.

I ran over and dropped to my knees. My hands slid over him, checking his broken body for mortal wounds. The shattered legs and wings were obvious. But, with his super-fast healing, neither would be life-threatening.

"Gren!" His face was a mask of blood, his arms covered

in claw marks that were so deep I was pretty sure I was seeing bone in some spots. And his beautiful wings...

Tears filled my eyes. I wrapped my fingers around his hand, feeling the warm slide of blood beneath my palm. Monty snuggled up next to Gren, tucking his long nose beneath the fallen protector's chin as if to comfort him.

"What can we do?" I asked Mavis, Bev, and Ferral.

In a heated wash of silver energy, Ferral's human form replaced the sleek moon hound. "He must be taken to a healer," the advocate said. He touched my shoulder with a warm hand. "Let me take him, Madam Lares."

I shook my head, the tears making the world swim around me. "I'm staying with him."

"We need your help, honey," Mavis said, her gaze sliding to Ferral's. "We need to get these two behind bars before they wake up."

I nodded. "Okay, do that. Thank you," I said as an afterthought as the harshness of my words sank in.

"Honey," Mavis said gently. "We need *you* to speak to Davis."

"Davis?" I shook my head. What did Rome's top cop have to do with anything? "I don't understand. Just tell him what you need."

"He's human, Aggy," Bev told me. "*You're* going to have to explain to him what's going on."

I finally looked up at them, my patience wearing thin. "You can tell him."

They shook their heads, Bev's expression turning angry. "This is your protectorate, Madam Lares. Only you can reveal magic to humans. That's the magical law."

When I shook my head again, my hand tightening around Gren's limp fingers. "The law be damned. Gren will die if I don't get him some help."

"Davis won't believe us. Only the Lares' magic will get through to him," Bev said.

I glanced at Ferral, not hearing them. "Can you carry him?"

"Yes, but..."

"Agnes Bethany Lenore!" Mavis barked out.

I blinked in surprise as my surrogate mom lost her temper. Mavis never lost her temper.

"You are the Lares of the *entire* town of Rome, Aggy. Not just of the select few you like. Everyone in Rome is currently in danger. You need to do your job to protect them all."

I closed my eyes, my fingers clenching as I struggled to accept that she was right. It wasn't about what I wanted.

After a moment, I nodded and stood, looking at Ferral. "You'll get him to a healer?"

Ferral inclined his head. Before I could change my mind, he scooped Gren up and threw him over one broad shoulder, then took off running like he wasn't carrying two hundred pounds of broken protector.

I threw Mavis and Bev a look that could have been warmer. "I'll go talk to Davis."

Hurt flared in Mavis's eyes. It tugged an answering regret from me. But I shoved the guilt away. I needed to deal with the problem at hand. That alone seemed an almost insurmountable goal, given that I could barely breathe through the panic of losing my friend.

I'd just have to take it a minute, and a single heavy step, at a time.

THE ROME POLICE Station consisted of a small "office" whose entrance was in an alley at the end of the street. The single room where Chief Davis Marshal greeted the public was small and dark, with no windows and very little attention paid to furnishings. There was no need for what the cop would consider "frou-frou." Davis was rarely in the office. He did his best work out on the streets. The people of Rome rarely visited his little, almost literal, hole in the wall.

During the day, the chief ran Rome on his own. Nights and weekends, two cops on loan from a nearby town covered for him, handling everything that wasn't delicate, political, or personal for Davis. When something seemed to fit those parameters, the part-time cops called Davis at home and he joined them at the scene.

That was the way it had been for as long as I could remember. As long as Davis was the chief cop in Rome, I didn't expect it would change.

I looked around the dimly lit room, my nose wrinkling as a sour smell stung my nostrils. A glance at the trash can next to the desk told me the smell probably came from one of the carry-out containers filling the can. It was definitely time to empty that trash.

The floor beneath my feet was covered in wide planks in a dark wood of indeterminate origin. The floor's polish had long ago worn down to a dull, muddy finish that rolled like a wave in some spots and was badly scratched in others. It creaked as I came inside and stepped back to hold the door wide for the first of two gurneys bearing our demon-possessed victims.

Imagine my surprise when I'd learned that Mavis kept gurneys at her house. She also, apparently, had medical supplies and a radio she used to call an ambulance when phones were out, as they often were during storm season. She used to work at Rome General Hospital, drove a car big enough to fit a gurney in the back, and, given the fact that the small, country hospital boasted only two ambulances that were usually unavailable when needed, I was guessing Mavis might have served as a backup EMT for Rome General a time or two.

I knew she had the skills to be a med tech. I'd watched her expertly treat and bandage the wounds I'd sustained fighting the demons before she'd allow me to came to talk to Davis.

Since I'd become Lares, the things I'd learned about my mom had been a constant surprise.

The big desk facing the door was made of a wood. It was old, but beautifully crafted, with dark grain under a reddish-gold stain. The desk's pristine surface held a small laptop sitting on an old-fashioned paper blotter and not much else.

Two plain wooden visitor chairs faced the desk.

A folding table on the wall to the right of the desk held a pot and fixings for coffee, along with real mugs instead of the usual Styrofoam cups.

Davis Marshal was an old-fashioned guy with craggy good looks. He was known for his sense of fairness, strong work ethic, and traditional values. Davis was a nice guy and a darn good cop.

He was also missing in action when we came through the door.

Monty wasted no time running over to sniff the floor around the table with the coffee. I had no doubt he was searching out crumbs to fill his empty belly. The poor thing had never gotten his breakfast. He probably thought he was dying.

The wall opposite the coffee center held a door. Next to the door on the wall was a series of hooks, each hook holding a different key.

A little further down the wall, a small grandfather clock

ticked away the time. It was a comforting sound, albeit one that seemed out of place in a police office.

A beat later, a flushing noise explained why the chief was missing.

We waited as the sound of running water, followed by the harsh belching of a hand dryer filled the silence.

The man who came out of the small bathroom in the back corner of the office jolted to a surprised stop when he saw us. "Oh." He frowned at the two gurneys. "What's going on? Do those people need an ambulance?"

Rome's one-and-only full-time cop was dressed in a flannel shirt and jeans, his sharp gaze and chiseled features easily identifying him as a cop, despite his casual dress.

Davis didn't wear a gun unless he was called out to a crime he thought would get violent, and his shield was usually stuffed into the pocket of his shirt.

With his thick mop of dark hair, graying on the sides, and tall, leanly muscled body, Davis was a good-looking guy and still solid despite his sixty-some years.

Like most people living in Rome, Davis Marshal might be relaxed about the way he dressed, but he was addicted to the rules of life in the small town. Everything had its place. Things were done a certain way. And life held no surprises except for the universally accepted things like death and, sometimes, taxes.

I was about to rock his world. I felt bad about that.

"Hey, Davis." I motioned toward the gurneys. Mavis and Bev each stood with a hand on a possessed's chest, no doubt feeding their spell with magic to keep the couple unconscious. "We brought some prisoners." I glanced around the office, my gaze falling to the door with the keys next to it. "Do you want us to take them directly to a cell?"

He frowned. "Prisoners?" He walked over and stood

between the two gurneys. "That's the Thomas's." He turned his frown on me. "What kind of crime did they commit?"

"They attacked two people in the street," Bev said, frowning as Davis turned her way. "It was a particularly gruesome attack."

Davis put his hands on his hips and shook his head. "That girl there..." He jerked his head toward the woman. "...she was on the cheerleading squad with my Delilah. She doesn't have a mean bone in her body."

Mavis and Bev looked at me. It was time to do my thing. I sighed. "Davis, you should probably take a seat."

He shook his head again. "I'm fine where I am." He stepped closer to the man on the gurney, bending down to examine his arm. "Those look like dog bites." He glared at us. "What's really going on here?"

I grabbed a chair from in front of the Police Chief's desk and pushed it toward him. Sending my energy into the air around Davis, I gave him what I hoped was a reassuring smile. "Sit, Chief. Please?"

He held my gaze for a long moment, his belligerent expression finally softening. He nodded and sat. I pulled the second chair over and sat down in front of him. The golden glow of my magic flowed from me to him, his body relaxing under its influence. "Chief, these people are demon-possessed. They need to be locked up until we can figure out how to get the demons out of them."

He narrowed his gaze on me. "Demons don't exist, Aggy." He glanced at Mavis. "Why are you letting her spread such nonsense around?"

If I remembered correctly, Mavis and Davis had gone to high school together. They might have even dated. Though, if high school during their time was anything like the high school years I'd barely survived, the name rhyming thing would have definitely been a problem for them.

I'd expected Mavis to look embarrassed by the question. I'd underestimated her. "Because she's telling you the truth, Davis. If you'd open that notoriously impenetrable mind of yours, you'd see that."

He shook his head.

"Demons do exist," I said, giving my energy an extra little push. I watched it hit him, turning his gaze dull and unfocused. *Oops! Too much.*

I reduced the pressure until his gaze sharpened. Then I tried again. "Magic exists, Chief. Magical creatures exist. It would be nice if we could ignore them, but circumstances have made that impossible."

"What kind of circumstances?" he asked, belligerence tightening his craggy features.

"A Hellmouth," I said, noting the hard glint in his dark blue eyes. Chief Marshal was no pushover. He was clearly resisting my influence. "At Golden Years Senior Home. It's a very dangerous situation, and I'm afraid these two young people might be the first victims of it."

Davis turned to stare at the couple, his brow lowering. "They look sick. They should be at the hospital."

Worry tightened my chest. What if I couldn't get him to understand? I'd already told him that magic was real. If I wasn't successful in getting him on board, I had probably just created a big problem. "Chief, they're not sick. They're possessed." When he shook his head, I tried another tack. "How about this. You help us get them locked up in a special cell. They're currently under a spell that the demons will push through quickly once Bev and Mavis stop reinforcing it. Then you can see what we're talking about."

His frown deepened. He stared at me for a long moment, clearly trying to read the level of madness in my eyes.

"She's telling you the truth, Davis," Mavis told him.

Finally, he sighed. "I'll humor you for a few minutes. But if those people still look sick after a few minutes in the cell, I'm calling an ambulance."

I slid a glance toward Mavis, and she winked.

I took that to mean it would be okay. "Fine. You do have a special cell, right?" According to Gren, who'd pronounced himself my teacher in all things magic and Rome, the previous Chief of Police in Rome had known about magical creatures and had a cell with iron bars on the sides and top and a stone floor beneath it. The cell had been infused with nulling magics, which were regularly reinforced by the town's local coven.

I glanced at Bev. "How long since the cell's been reinforced?"

"Just last week," my sister of the heart said. "After your seating, we figured we'd better be prepared for whatever came."

"Good call," I mumbled, a shudder sliding over me at the memory. I'd been late to the party, so to speak, in knowing about magic in general, and my magic in particular.

Davis unlocked the door leading to the cells and slipped the key back into his pocket. He grabbed a skeleton key from the hooks beside the door and flipped a light switch on the wall. A long hallway was illuminated. Its walls were plain concrete block and the floor was poured concrete.

He glanced at the gurneys. "Do you ladies need help with those?"

"It might be better to have someone at the head and foot since we'll be maneuvering down the hall," Bev said.

Eyeing the musty-smelling space, I saw her point. The floor was uneven in spots. The cracked concrete had heaved from moisture over the years, as well as the normal shifting of an aging building.

Monty started to trot through the door, but I grabbed his trailing leash. "Not so fast, mister. You need to stay here where it's safe."

He barked, his tail manically smacking the air.

"I know," I told him. "But that's just the way it is." Looping the handle of the leash around a chair leg, I went to help Bev with her gurney. Davis sent me an amused glance as I passed him. "What?" I asked the chief.

He grinned. "Do you always talk to that dog like he understands you?"

"Of course. Because he does."

Davis's smile sagged. His eyes went round. "Are you telling me he's a magical dog?"

I fought a grin. I might have laid on the suggestion a bit too thick. "I'm not sure. But he's definitely special."

Shaking his head, Davis went to help Mavis with her gurney. "I've had dogs all my life," he told me in a grumpy voice. "Almost every single one ate poop and rocks. If that's the kind of special you mean, then I guess I'd have to agree."

I shook my head, grinning.

The chief and Mavis went first, the chief moving quickly as if he were anxious to get the whole thing over with.

I bit back a sigh. My influence might have softened him up to the whole "magic exists" thing, but it hadn't helped his mood even a tiny bit.

The concrete beneath my feet was cold as we made our way along the dimly lit space. The bare bulb in the center of the passage was overwhelmed by the windowless space of the hallway, a fact not helped by the high, narrow windows in the cell area beyond.

When we emerged from the passage a moment later, I found myself looking at a dungeon-like space that didn't appear to have ever been updated since its origin. I wouldn't have been too surprised to see metal rings on the walls with rusty chains extending to the floor.

"Charming," I said, without considering the company I kept.

Davis's broad shoulders squared, and his eyes hardened. "I don't believe in coddling prisoners, Aggy."

"Clearly." I grimaced, thinking about the occasional shop-lifting teen or falsely arrested person being locked up in there. The experience would definitely leave a scar.

Davis pointed to the largest cell, which held two cots, a stainless steel toilet, and a small sink. "In here." We rolled the two people onto the cots and left. Davis used the strange, old-fashioned key to lock the cell. The chief probably didn't realize it, but Gren had told me the previous police chief had the skeleton key magically created by witches so that it could never be copied or the lock on the cell picked.

As the lock clicked into place, a low-level hum filled the air, and a soft, green glow coated the entire cell.

Davis blinked at the sight as if he'd never seen it before.

That was when I realized my push had probably worked after all. At least on some level. It hadn't adjusted his understanding of the situation, but it had apparently opened his eyes to magic.

"What's going on?"

"Magic," I told him with a smile. "That cell has been reinforced to ensure the prisoners inside can't use energy or exceptional strength to escape."

He turned to Bev and Mavis. "What was in that blessing you all gave these cells last week?"

"Aggy already told you. Reinforcing magic. Stop being so stubborn," Mavis said.

"Miss Mavis," he said, fondness painting his tone, "I learned a long time ago that words mean nothing. I believe what I see with my own eyes and hear with my own ears."

The man on the cot stirred, his eyes suddenly snapping open. They glowed a deep, blood-red.

I grimaced. "You're about to see with your own eyes, Chief."

He sighed as if my presence was annoying him. It probably was. He'd be darn lucky if he walked out of that room simply annoyed and not terrorized by what he was about to see.

The man on the cot flew toward us so fast he was nothing more than a blur on the air. He slammed into the bars of the cell near ceiling height, clinging to it like a giant spider.

Chief Davis Marshal took two steps back, his eyes wide and his mouth open. "Holy..."

"There's nothing holy about that, Chief," Bev said, her lips curved in a tight smile.

The man in the cell opened his mouth and spat something black and slimy all over the front of Davis and me. Bev jumped away with a yelp, and Mavis ducked behind her gurney. Before I could react, I caught movement out of the corner of my eye, and the cell bars clanged as the woman joined the man. I watched in horror as she clambered over the bars like a giant arachnid, growling in a voice that was way too deep for a human being.

Davis stood with his arms arched away from his body.

Slimy black stuff oozed down his shirt and dripped onto the floor. He hadn't moved since getting hit with the nasty stuff.

"Believe us now, Chief?" I asked.

He didn't respond at first, slowly turning his gaze to mine. "What's wrong with them?"

Mavis rolled her eyes. Bev sighed. I started to pat him on the shoulder and then stopped, grimacing at the mess. "Demons. Those people can't be let out of that cell, Chief. Not until we figure out how to get rid of the demons."

He scrubbed a hand over his chin, scraping off a slimy strand of demon spit. "I understand."

And I believed he finally did.

We turned away and started back toward the office. As we reached the door, a horrendous squealing sound jolted us to a stop.

I looked at Bev and Mavis. "Did that sound like metal bending to you?"

"Goddess save us," Bev breathed out. "It did."

Another squeal had us turning on our heels and running back to the magically reinforced cell. We arrived just in time to see the man shoving his shoulder through a ten-inch gap between the bars. He was a big guy, broad in the shoulders and kind of meaty, but his bones must have compressed somehow because he'd managed to squash a quarter of his body through the opening before we could react.

Without thought, I opened my mind and sent a 9-1-1 call into the ether.

We were about to be overwhelmed by what was coming at us. And I was pretty sure we needed a lot of help.

8

A GOOD MAN FALLS, A GUARDIAN WEEPS

I turned to Davis. "Get weapons. Anything you can find. And, whatever you do, don't let them out of this room if they manage to get past us."

He nodded and started running.

I looked at Bev and Mavis. They were already spinning magic in the air. The strands of glowing energy knitted themselves into something that looked like an advanced math equation to me. I had no idea what they did when they crafted a spell. For all I knew, it *could* be math-based.

The woman inside the cell snarled. I turned to find the two demons fighting for access to the single opening. The man still had one arm and a shoulder through, but the woman was clawing and biting at him, trying to yank him out so she could escape.

Whatever they'd been to each other during their lives, the poison invading their bodies had killed any humanity they'd once had.

With a terrifying speed that created a blur on the air, the woman was thrown back and the man shot through the dented bars. He slammed into me, sending us both flying backward. I hit the bars of the cell across the room, the sound echoing through the stark space.

Agony speared through my back and neck. A galaxy of stars created sparkly little spots in my vision, obscuring part of the nightmare that was snapping at my face.

I fought to stay conscious. If I passed out, the teeth snapping at my face and the long, black claws the demon had grown since taking over the human man's form would rip me into tiny little pieces.

In a move that was more desperation than skill, I smacked the demon on the side of the face and sent energy spearing through his skull. His head jerked to the side, but the jolt of power didn't seem to have much more effect than that.

A shrill scream brought my head whipping around to find the female clinging to Bev, her teeth buried in my sister's shoulder as Bev stumbled backward.

Screaming with fear and rage, I all but levitated from the floor and threw out my hands. "Expel!" The single command was edged in panic, my voice shrill above the snarling and screaming.

The female flew away from Bev, her body folded in on itself as it crashed through the open doorway of another cell.

Mavis flung her hands out, and the glowing mesh of magic she'd been building hit the door of the cell and slammed it shut, wrapping around the entire iron cage like a huge mesh bandage.

The woman pinged right off the back of the cell and flew toward the door, hitting it hard enough to rattle the entire structure. She howled and snarled, slimy black spittle coating the bars and the floor beyond.

But the spell seemed to hold.

The male lunged toward Mavis, his running lope and sagging jaw reminding me of a cross between a large ape and a zombie. His red eyes glowed brighter as he zeroed in on my family.

That was it. I was so over demons. Done. Narrowing my gaze on the monster as his clawed feet left the ground, I gathered all the magic in my core with a thought and flung it in his direction. The energy flew away from me in an unfocused wave, slamming into the male and enshrouding him in a sizzling wash of power that held him locked into place mere inches from Bev and Mavis. The building groaned under the force of the rabid energy and rocked on its foundation, dust sifting down on our heads.

Still, the demon fought my control, managing to move a foot and the fingers of one hand within seconds. I wouldn't be able to hold him for long.

I looked at my mom and sister. "Get out!" I screamed, my voice reverberating unnaturally around the room.

"We're not leaving you," Mavis screamed back.

One of the demon's arms wrenched free of my hold and his hand shot toward Mavis, the clawed fingers wrapping around her throat. The demon lifted her off the ground as she clawed at his fingers. Her eyes bulged and her mouth worked, fighting to draw air into her lungs.

Bev threw another spell at the creature. It hit him in the face like a giant fist. He staggered back but held onto Mavis.

Bev threw herself at him, clawing at his eyes. I wrapped an arm around his neck from the back and tried to choke him out. If we could get the human body to pass out, we might have time to restrain the demons before they woke up again.

A door slammed in the distance, and heavy footsteps pounded toward us. "Get down!" Davis yelled.

Bev and I dropped just as the cop shot the male in the neck with a large dart. Mavis was purple in the face, and she was going limp.

I knew we had only seconds.

I looked at Davis. "Blade!"

He reached into his waistband and yanked out what looked like a hunting blade. It was ten inches long with a serrated edge. He slid it across the floor in my direction.

I snatched it up and, before I could think about what I was doing, slashed down on the demon's wrist, infusing the blow with energy.

With a howl of pain that had an all-too-human edge to it, The demon staggered back, its bleeding stump of an arm clutched in one hand. Mavis sagged toward the floor, but Bev caught her before she hit her head.

Davis shot another dart into the demon as it stumbled, trying to renew its attack.

"Get her out of here," I told Bev. She nodded, finally realizing the wisdom of my suggestion.

Thank the goddess.

"I'll be back after I get her to safety."

I shook my head but had no breath left to argue. My knees were like rubber, and my arms were weak. The adrenaline that had been keeping me afloat was starting to wane.

I was going to be as weak as a kitten by the time we got out of there.

The male was finally starting to succumb to the darts Davis had pumped into him. Unbelievably, it had taken five of the things to slow him down.

The chief was peppering the woman with darts as I watched, knife in hand in case he got into trouble.

My mind raced. We no longer had a spelled cage to keep

them in. I needed to get creative. I wracked my brain, looking for a solution.

Then it hit me, and I sent out a call to the only person I knew could help. *I need you.*

In the space of a single heartbeat, Reverend Dodson was floating up through the stone floor.

"Aggy?" His wispy form floated a few feet away, his gaze finding the possessed humans and narrowing. "Ah. Poor souls."

I wanted to agree. I'd felt the same way. Before. "We need to stop them from breaking out of here. The only hope of saving them is to keep them contained until we deal with the vortex."

He nodded, his hands folded serenely at his waist. He thought about it for a moment, his gaze sliding around the room. "You need a field of consecrated ground."

"Yes."

"Very smart."

"Thank you. I'm afraid we need to do it fast, though. We're having trouble keeping them down."

He nodded. "Alright then. I'll get started. Can you get me some things?"

"Of course." I pulled out my phone, tapping the notes app. "What do you need?"

A minute later, I called Bev to find out how Mavis was. "She's ticked off but fine," my sister told me, a smile in her voice. "It's all I can do to keep her from coming in there again."

"I have a job for you two that might keep her busy enough to forget about flinging herself at a demon."

"Good."

"Reverend Dodson is going to create a barrier of consecrated ground to keep the demons in the cell. He needs us to bring him these things. I rattled off the items on the screen, which included sanctified water, several large crosses, and a rosary. I'll text you the list. Can you get these things fast?"

"We'll be back as soon as we can."

"Thanks," I told her. I disconnected and watched the male twitch as if he were trying to wake up. Glancing at Davis, I asked. "How many more of those darts do you have?"

He snorted and shot another dart into the man. The demon-possessed went limp again. "Two more boxes. I'll go get them." He started toward the office and stopped, coming back to me. He pulled a gun from the back waistband of his jeans, handing it to me. "If all else fails."

I frowned but took it. The gun might kill the human hosts, which was exactly what I didn't want. But I couldn't keep chopping parts off of them either. I sighed, my choices limited. "Thanks. Can you help me pull him into the cell with the female before you leave? At least that will slow them down a bit if they wake up before you get back."

"Happy to. We should tie that arm off too. He'll probably lose it, but we can at least keep him from bleeding to death."

A few minutes later, I watched Davis leave, wishing I could go with him. But I couldn't leave. I was the only thing between the demons and the door. And goddess help me if it came down to me keeping them there by myself. I was almost too tired to stand.

With a sigh, I leaned back against the wall, not daring to sit for fear I'd fall asleep, and watched Reverend Dodson walk around the cell, clutching his ghostly rosary and softly chanting.

~

The door slamming at the end of the hall jerked me out of a doze. I straightened away from the wall and scrubbed at my face.

Footsteps moved down the hall toward me. I waited in silence, expecting to see Davis returning with more darts.

I couldn't have been more wrong.

It took me a moment to react to the seven-foot-tall creature with straight black horns that stuck out to the sides of its head and a narrow, triangular face. The creature's dove-gray skin had a scaled aspect to it, the scales more texture than actual scaling. The eyes, exotically slanted, were black with fiery centers. Its hands looked surprisingly delicate against the oversized body, and its legs were bent, like a goat's hind end, with split hooves like a farm animal.

A lost one!

Power bit at my fingertips as I drew energy without even thinking. But the creature stopped and folded its hands, cocking its strangely delicate head and staring at me through those unusual eyes. "I mean no harm."

The door slammed again, and footsteps pounded toward us. I held the energy, not wanting whoever it was to get caught in the crossfire. "I won't let you have them," I told the creature.

It shook its head, a halo of soft blonde hair swaying with the motion. I frowned at the hair...the calm demeanor...and the relative delicacy of the creature. "You're a lost one," I said.

It nodded. "Yes."

"You can't have these demons. If you try to take them, I'll have to kill you." I only hoped I could live up to my bluff.

Ferral emerged from the hallway, his movements tight with anger. Settling a snapping gaze on the lost one, he growled out. "I told you to wait for me in the office."

The creature's smile would have been more attractive if it wasn't filled with so many deadly teeth. "I was curious."

I glanced at Ferral. "You brought this thing here?"

The lost one's delicately slitted nostrils flared at my insult, but I didn't care. Her kind had attacked my people and me not too long ago, sending one of the people I was supposed to protect to the Elysium Fields. I'd carry his death and my failure to save him to my grave.

Ferral held up a hand, his angry expression turning on me. "Hold your magic and your judgment, Aggy," he said. "Let me explain."

I settled onto the balls of my feet, my energy firmly held at the ready. "I'm listening."

He frowned. "Remember when I told you earlier that I had a...situation?"

I nodded. "When I asked why you were gone for so long."

"Yes." He jerked his head toward the lost one. "The princess here *was* the situation I was referring to."

Well, that was as clear as tar. "Explain."

The "princess" cocked her head in his direction, a closed-mouth smile on her strange face. She appeared to be amused by his obvious struggle to explain her presence there.

The hall door slammed shut again. More footsteps. Davis's voice preceded him down the hall. "Sorry that took so long. I had to dig in my supply room to find more darts..." He jolted to a stop and paled, one big hand clutching a box and the other his dart gun. "What in the world?"

I held up a hand. "Don't shoot it, Davis. Ferral was just telling me why he brought it here."

The lost one's lips curved higher, exposing a mouth full of nasty teeth.

The chief turned another shade paler and took a step back. "Aggy."

"Yeah?" I said, watching him closely for signs that he was going to pass out.

"On the subject of that magic stuff you told me about?"

I cleared my throat and looked away so he wouldn't see me smile. "Yeah?"

"I believe you."

I chuckled then. I couldn't help it. "Thanks, Chief."

Looking back and forth between us, Ferral's brows lowered. "If we could get to the matter at hand?"

"I'm waiting on you for that," I told him, not fond of his judgy tone of voice.

"As I was saying, the princess surprised me out there. It took me a moment to understand that I was seeing a full-blown lost princess in Rome in broad daylight. By the time I'd gathered my wits about me..."

"What he's trying to say is that I kicked his furry butt," the princess interrupted.

I barked out a laugh when Ferral's arrogant face darkened to purple. "I believe I gave as good as I got."

She snorted, reminding me a lot of Wanda, which made me wonder how old she was.

"Yet here you both are," I said. "Together. In a protected place." I lifted my brows at Ferral, letting him know, in case he'd missed it, that I wasn't happy with his choice to bring the demonic creature to the jail when we already had our hands full with the two we had.

"She offered to help," he growled out.

"And you believed her?" I snapped back.

"Yes. I know you have a sour taste in your mouth from the lost ones we encountered before..."

"You could say that," I responded.

"Layla is different."

I crossed my arms and gave him the look my mom used to give me when I'd told her a whopper. Unfortunately, not having been blessed with kids, I hadn't been able to use it as much as I'd have liked. But I'd learned over the years that it was equally useful against men. I mean, since they were mostly like giant children. "You don't say?"

He glared at me, fuming.

I'll admit it. I was enjoying his discomfort. He was usually way too cool and collected for my taste.

"He is correct, Madam Lares," the princess said. "Have you not read our history?"

I hadn't, but I didn't want to admit that I was a newbie in the magical world. I already felt too much like an impostor as a guardian deity who had no clue how to guard or...deit. I winced. "I know that you've been cast out of the demonic realm, and you want to go back."

The creature held up one long finger with a thick claw at the end. Unbelievably, the claw was painted in a French manicure.

That made my eyes go wide.

"You speak of the lawless, lower castes," she told me. Her tone when speaking about the other lost ones sounded a lot like Ferral's. Judgy and a bit arrogant. "I am royalty. We do not wish to return to that inhospitable place. We are happy here."

I blinked in surprise. "Seriously?"

"Seriously," she verified.

I narrowed my gaze on her. "How many of you are there?"

Shrugging, she examined her claws with a critical eye. "I do not have an exact count. There are many."

Realizing she wasn't going to give me specifics, I asked, "You say you can help?"

She nodded.

"How?"

The princess strolled toward the cage that contained our demon-possessed couple. She moved with a surprisingly light step, given the awkward bend and heaviness of her legs. Reverend Dodson looked up as she passed him, inclining his head as if she weren't something from a person's worst nightmares.

The creature inclined her head in response. She stopped in front of the cell and slid a critical gaze over it. Then she reached out and touched the metal, creating a spark with her touch. She pulled her hand back, but not as quickly as I would have, given that her fingertip was smoking. "I will give you two of my people to guard the possessed."

I glanced at Ferral. He nodded. "They are unsurpassed in strength in their domain. They are less so here, in an unnatural habitat, but they are still stronger than the possessed."

The princess threw him a look filled with disdain. "I beat your furry butt pretty handily," she reminded him.

Ferral sighed. "Yes, Princess Layla. You beat my furry butt."

Her gaze sparkled with mischief. "I'm up for a rematch anytime."

My advocate stared at her a long moment, something sneaky slithering through his pretty silver eyes. Finally, he inclined his head, a slight smile curving his lips. "You're on. *After* we close the Hellmouth."

9

WHEN VIRTUE DARES AND EVIL SLEEPS

"So, about that vortex," I said, meeting the lost princess's gaze. "Can you close it?"

The creature shook her head without hesitation. "I cannot."

I waited for her to explain, but she didn't, so I glanced at Ferral.

"She's correct, Madam Lares. The lost ones cannot manipulate vortexes. If they could, they would no longer be lost."

I blinked at the simple logic in his statement. "Oh. Right." I sighed. "Okay, can I leave you to handle this, then? I need to get with the rest of the council and see if we can come up with a plan."

"Of course, Madam Lares."

"I'll see you later at home," I told Ferral. I collected Monty on my way out, passing Bev and Mavis on the stairs.

"Sorry we took so long," Bev said when she saw me. "We had trouble getting holy water. Saint Paul church is locked." She frowned. "Father Ignacious never closes it. Something must be wrong there."

I bit back a sigh. She was right. I'd need to check on him. "Did you find the water?"

Mavis nodded. "The Lutheran church had some." She glanced toward the door. "You're leaving? Does that mean the prisoners are secure?"

"Sort of?"

"Was that a question?" Bev asked.

"Kind of?"

Bev moved a jar of water and shifted some candles, looking harried. "Spill, Agnes."

I sighed. The full name thing meant she was cranky. "Ferral brought us a lost princess. She says she'll give us two of her people to guard the possessed."

Mavis and Bev shared a look before pinning me with a dual glare. "And you just left that thing in there? It will release them as soon as we're not looking. They're all demons."

Technically, the lost ones were devils, but I figured it was a distinction without a difference. I shook my head. "Ferral seems very sure that it's a good idea." Descending to street level, I stopped with my hand on the knob, turning back to them. "Can your coven exorcise the demons from that couple in there?"

Bev and Mavis shared a look. "We already tried, honey," Mavis said. "While I was dressing your wounds Bev did an exorcism spell. It didn't work."

I frowned. "Why not?"

Bev shrugged. "We don't know. We're looking into it." She didn't look as if she had much hope they'd find a solution in time. I didn't disagree with her. The demons had done a lot of damage to the Thomas's in a short time.

"Okay," I said, disappointment burrowing deep. "Keep me posted on that." I yanked the door open.

"Wait, honey," Mavis called out as I pushed the door open. "Where are you going?"

"I need to check on the residents at Golden Years. I didn't have time to do it because we had to rush here to stop three demons. Then I need to check on the priest at Saint Paul. Then somebody needs to monitor the town in case more of those things show up."

Just listing everything that needed to be done made me exhausted.

"Okay, I get it. But you have a council for a reason," Mavis said. "Use us."

She was right. "Yeah. Okay. I'll do that. Can one of you break into the church and check on Father Ignacious?"

Bev nodded. "Let me just get this stuff to the Rev, and I'll go do that."

"What do you want me to do?" Mavis asked.

"Stay with Ferral in case he needs help? Then let everybody know we need to meet at my house tonight." I frowned as I realized having everybody there would require that I feed them. "We'll need food. Can you call for pizzas?"

"Let me handle the food. You shouldn't go back to the senior home without backup. Is Gren back yet?"

My eyes burned. I realized I'd been so discombobulated by the princess's arrival, I'd forgotten to ask Ferral about Gren. "I don't know. I doubt it. That homeless demon really beat him up."

"Isn't a homeless demon the same thing as a lost one?" Bev asked with a sly smile.

I rubbed my temple as a headache pulsed there. "I don't know. I'm so confused."

"Call Luke or Trish then," Mavis said, giving Bev a look for teasing me. "Have one of them go with you. I'll contact

Niele and have him stay in town to monitor the demon situation."

I felt all the blood leave my face. "Make him wear pants!" I could just see him walking around Rome with his dangly bits waving around.

Bev snorted out a laugh. "Of course."

Trish had come directly from work. Sawdust coated her fine blonde hair, and she still wore her tool belt draped low on her narrow hips. I eyed the hammer hanging from the belt and wondered if it would be any use against a demon.

Probably not. But Trish's warrior magic would give us some protection if the worst should happen.

Monty trotted ahead of us into the senior home. His built-in dachshund confidence was on full display. I wished I had even a fraction of his cockiness at the moment. It would at least have been nice if my knees weren't knocking together.

"Where's the vortex?" Trish asked, her bright green gaze sliding around the lobby.

I pointed toward the large windows overlooking the courtyard, frowning. The maelstrom had grown so big I could see part of it from the lobby. "I'll show you. I should check on it anyway."

I left Monty in the lobby, and Trish followed me outside. She sucked in a breath as she saw the enormity of the roiling, inky hole. Her gaze slid upward and she gasped again. "Who's that?"

"Shadee. She's the night nurse here. From what she's told me, she has a voodoo queen in her family. I don't know if she's the one who brought this horror to life or if the vortex just sensed the magic in her blood. Either way, it's currently drawing energy from her."

I moved closer and eyed the poor woman. Shadee looked smaller than the last time I'd seen her. Her body had twisted slightly as if the vortex was wringing her out.

"That's horrible," Trish said, grimacing. "Shouldn't we help her?"

"I intend to. But Ferral doesn't think it's safe to try to remove her while the vortex is active."

We stood in silence, each caught up in our own thoughts. Or, in my case, fears.

"Give me a second," Trish said a moment later, removing her tool belt and laying it in the grass. I blinked in surprise as she popped into her fairy form. She hovered in front of me, her translucent wings glowing a pale green. She was about twelve inches tall and was wearing a long gown in lieu of her usual jeans and tee shirt. The dress fluttered around her legs and featured a bright blue bustier with a belt of knives. She held a knobby staff that was as tall as she was, and there was an opaline orb at the top that I knew flared with jagged bolts of silver lightning. A double strand of what looked like shimmering water droplets encircled her blonde head.

She shot away from me, circling Shadee and occasionally sending a silver spray of energy from the orb on her staff to wash over the other woman, as if she were assessing Shadee's condition.

Apparently satisfied with what she found, she hovered low over the vortex, the glow from her staff sliding over the oily black energy, which bubbled with agitation wherever her magic touched it.

She flew back to me and returned to her human form in

a flash of silver light, her delicate features formed into an unhappy expression.

"What's wrong?" I asked.

"That woman isn't just related to a voodoo queen," she told me, casting a thoughtful look in Shadee's direction. "She's about as powerful a practitioner as I've ever seen."

My eyes went wide. "Really?"

"Really." Trish slid a worried gaze my way. "If the vortex is getting its strength from her, we're in deep trouble. She's strong enough to fuel a whole lot of destruction."

"Curse!" I said with feeling. "That's just wonderful."

Trish nodded.

"Okay, well, there's nothing we can do about it at the moment. But it's good to know exactly what we're working with here."

"There's more," Trish said. "I don't know if you're aware of this, but...every time something passes through the vortex, it leaves behind an energy scar, like a pockmark on the surface."

I tensed, fearing I knew precisely where she was going with that bit of information. "Okay."

Trish's gaze found the vortex again, lingering on the bubbling, swirling surface. "From the number of scars I'm seeing there, we probably have close to a dozen demons lingering in the area. One of them was really powerful."

I was pretty sure I'd met that one already. So had Gren. I scrubbed my hands over my face. "Swear, curse, swear."

"My sentiments exactly," Trish agreed.

"How are they coming through if the vortex hasn't reached full power yet?" I asked.

She shrugged. "I can't give you the how or why, but I know it's possible."

"Great," I said, sighing. "We've already bumped up

against three of them, and they kicked our butts from here to next week," I said. "If we're going to survive this whole mess, we're going to need to find a better way to fight them."

"Have you used your staff?"

I bit back a groan. "Not recently. But last week, I blew up a tree in the yard with it. So...there's that."

Trish grinned at me. "Would you like some training?"

I stared at her for a moment. "You could train me?"

"Of course. You might have noticed, I use one myself."

She did at that. And I'd much rather work with Trish than ask my dad for help. Even though he was well aware of what a train wreck I was, given the fact that I came to the whole ancient guardian deity thing really late in life and had a steep learning curve ahead, I still didn't want him to know what a mess I was with the pretty stick. "I'd be forever in your debt."

"Good." Trish shoved her hands into the pockets of her well-worn jeans. "Let's check on those residents then. Mavis texted me that we were due at your place for dinner in two hours. And she's making lasagna."

10

WITH DANGEROUS ALLIES AT HER SIDE

The residence wing was eerily quiet. As we stood listening just inside the door, I tried to remember what Shadee had told me about the ones who remained in the building. She'd spoken about a man who'd survived the deadly vortex squeal because he was deaf. What had his name been? Pintwalls? Pintwallen. That was it. And there'd been a woman too. Mrs...Wolde. Shadee had described Mrs. Wolde as being extremely shy.

I turned to Trish. "We're looking for two people. Mrs. Wolde and Mr. Pintwallen. The man is hard of hearing and she might be too shy to announce herself."

"Got it," Trish said. "I'll go that way?"

Nodding, I said, "I'll head in the other direction. The place is built in a large oval surrounding the courtyard. I'll meet you on the other side."

Most of the doors were open. I assumed those were the rooms where Shadee had found injured residents. I made a quick foray into each small apartment, checking closets and bathrooms if the main living space was empty, which was the case in all of them.

Monty's tail wagged with happy enthusiasm as he put himself into adventure mode again. He bounced from room to room with me, scouring crumbs off the floor and sniffing everything in sight.

Despite my dog's happy attitude, by the time I reached the first of three communal spaces, my mood had darkened, a deep sadness settling in to weigh me down. The place had a dystopian, abandoned feeling, as if a zombie hoard had come along and chased everybody out.

Seemingly reacting to my mood, Monty plopped down next to me, so close his little body was pressed against my ankle.

The seating areas all looked exactly the same, which seemed like it would be disorienting to the residents. But maybe they took comfort in the familiarity. Each space had one wall with built-in book shelves, which were filled with well-used paper and hard-cover books. A long, upholstered couch faced an electric fireplace that I knew from experience turned the room uncomfortably warm when in use. Five armchairs, two of which were covered in the same flowered chintz as the couch and three in complimenting shades to match the chintz, were arranged to face the couch. There was no coffee table in the center of the seating, probably to provide an open space that wheelchairs could easily traverse.

A large screen television hung on the wall above the electric fireplace. As always, a local news program played on the TV, the sound muted.

As in the lobby, a wall of large windows, with glass doors, led to the courtyard. I glanced toward the windows, reluctant to look at the scene beyond the glass because I still had no idea how to deal with the growing problem.

From where I stood, I had a different vantage point of

poor Shadee. I stared at her floating body from the side rather than head on, and noticed that her fingers were curved downward, a thin strand of energy flowing into the abyss from their tips.

The strands leading from her fingertips appeared to pulse downward, where the strands I'd spotted earlier seemed to rise from the glossy surface of the nightmare beneath her.

Was it possible that Shadee was somehow manipulating the energy of the maelstrom?

I shivered, rubbing my arms as a chill swept through the room. Gooseflesh beaded my arms. Ice slipped along my spine.

Monty growled, low and deep, and fur stood up along his back.

A soft, whispery sigh wafted through the air behind me. A touch, ethereal and fleeting, skittered along my neck. I whipped around, my heart pounding.

A shadow danced across the wall. The skirt of the couch twitched, and the pull chain on the floor lamp next to it swung violently from side to side.

Panic flared as I realized the room had grown darker. Much too dark for late afternoon. My gaze slid to the sky beyond the glass, where thick charcoal clouds had moved in front of the sun. A gust of rabid wind made Shadee's robe dance and tossed her hair around her face.

Another whispered sigh. Fear danced along my nerves. Energy nibbled at my fingertips. I whipped around again, "Trish?" I called out hopefully.

The room seemed to wobble, the floor beneath my feet shifting. I stumbled forward, barely catching myself on the back of an upholstered chair as the glooms reached toward me from the edges of the room. A cacophony of whispering voices seemed to draw them forward.

I forced my racing pulse to slow, my ears straining to recognize the words floating past on an increasingly frigid breeze.

"Who's there?"

The whispering got louder, dancing from one place to another, pulling my gaze with it as it moved.

My skin crawled.

Monty's growls were constant, the tenor fierce.

My stomach twisted as terror tied it into knots, and I looked down to find magic snapping at my fingertips. I was all amped up with nowhere to go.

"Shush, Monty," I said in a harsh whisper. Amazingly, he listened to me. But his little body vibrated with nerves.

"Aggy?" a welcome voice called out from down the hall.

As if a light switch had been flipped, the eerie whispers died. The blustery drafts fell away, and the sun emerged again from the clouds.

With a yip of excitement, Monty ran toward the voice.

"Aggy? Where are you?" Trish's worried voice approached from the resident wing ahead.

"I'm here." I hurried forward, just as eager to leave whatever that was behind me as I was to speak to an actual human being again.

Trish was moving slowly toward us down the hall. I was happy to see that she was towing a small, gnarled man with bowed legs and very poor balance along with her.

She looked relieved when she saw me, the tension in her posture softening. "Thank the goddess. I thought I'd lost you."

"Eh!" shouted the little man. "What's that?"

Trish grimaced as he shouted into her ear, giving me a long-suffering look.

"Nothing, Mr. Pintwallen," Trish screamed back from inches away. She'd yelled her response so loudly, it blew the wispy hairs on the top of his round head flat against his skull.

Still, he hadn't seemed to hear.

"Huh? You got to speak up, girlie. I told ya that." Monty jumped up and licked across the man's sweatpants-covered knee, earning himself a scowl from the cranky old man and a swipe of one impatient hand.

Trish looked at me and sighed. "Any luck finding Mrs. Wolde?"

"No." I frowned. "She wasn't in any of the rooms from the lobby to here."

Trish stared at me. "This is as far as you got? What happened?"

"I'm not sure." I rubbed my arms again. "Something was...here."

She looked around, her gaze narrowing on the shadowed places. "Is it still here?"

"I don't think so. Did you check the other rooms after you found Mr. Pintwallen?"

"Dangnabit!" the old man yelled unhappily. "I told ya to speak up. All that whisperin' is just frustratin'. I don't know why young people can't speak in a normal tone of voice."

Trish and I shared a smile. "Come on," I said. "Let's go check the rest of the rooms."

~

OVER AN HOUR LATER, we still hadn't found the other resident. I'd even tried to check the basement, though the idea of going down there after what I'd experienced in the common area gave me hives. The basement door was locked, which meant that we weren't the only ones who couldn't access that space.

"Mrs. Wolde wouldn't have been able to get down there," Trish said, mirroring my thoughts. "Unless she could get to the lobby or the nurse's room?"

I shook my head. "These residents are all suffering some kind of dementia. They lock all the staff spaces to keep them safe." A.k.a. keep them from escaping.

I grimaced at the thought of being confined that way. Logically, I realized that it truly was for the residents' safety. But it would be horrible to have my free will taken away like that.

"She must have gotten out somehow," I mused, unhappy at the idea.

"You're sure she wasn't in the group that went to the hospital?"

I shook my head. "Shadee said she wasn't. But I guess she could have made a mistake. Unfortunately, we can't ask her about it."

"Well, she's not here. What should we do with Mr. Pintwallen? We can't leave him here. It's not safe."

We both looked at the elderly man sitting on the couch. He was staring at the muted television screen. Strangely, he didn't seem to mind that he couldn't hear it.

Trish glanced around. "It's strange that none of the other staff has shown up."

I shook my head. "After we got everyone into the ambulances this morning, Shadee called someone and told them not to let anyone come to the facility until she gave them the all-clear. She made up a story about a highly infectious outbreak or something" I'd been only half listening at the time. "I have a feeling she gave her request a little extra oomph if you know what I mean."

Trish nodded. "That doesn't help us with our Mr. Pintwallen problem."

"Eh?" the old man shouted.

She grinned.

"We can take him to the Sunflower Ranch in Benson," I said, warming to the idea. The ranch was a physical rehabilitation facility about thirty miles away. When I'd worked at Golden Years, I'd often driven residents to the facility for physical therapy. "I'll give them a call and clear it. Can you drive him over?"

"Of course," Trish said. She walked over and held out her hands to the elderly man. He looked at her hands for a beat and then took them, allowing her to gently pull him to his feet.

"Where we goin', young lady?"

Trish leaned very close and bellowed into his ear. "I'm taking you for a vacation. You'd like that, right?"

"Eh?" he bellowed back. "What's that now?"

"Goddess in garters," Trish mumbled as she led him toward the exit.

"I'll see you at my house," I called out to her. "Come on, sweet boy," I told my dog. "Let's go home and get you some dinner." On the way home, I'd make my call to the Sunflower Ranch. Then I'd call Davis and have him search for Mrs. Wolde. Hopefully, the missing resident hadn't gotten far.

Monty gave a happy woof that made me envy his joie de vivre. Nothing in Heaven or Hell seemed to put a crimp in the little dog's sense of adventure.

~

WHEN I HEARD the front door slam, I glanced up at the clock. Wanda was right on schedule.

"Hello?" the teen called out, her tone lighter than usual. "Anybody here?"

I winced, knowing the girl didn't have many carefree moments in her bespelled life. I hated to rob her of one of them. But I didn't see any way around it. I needed her help. "In the kitchen," I answered.

Monty ran toward the front door, a happy bounce in his step. Over the weeks since I'd accepted my legacy as Lares and gained a council to help me do my job, Wanda and my dog had formed a close attachment with each other. More than his relationship with every other member of my team, that growing closeness made me happy. I doubted Wanda had ever had a dog of her own. Since being bespelled by a witch who'd also stolen the teen's mother from her, she barely had a life of her own.

Wanda gave a soft squeal when she saw Monty. As usual, she spoke to my little hero in a quiet voice. I speculated it was because she didn't want me to hear the baby talk she used with him.

I grinned. The hard-case teen Gren and I had met for the first time foraging in my kitchen, bold as you please, barely ever surfaced anymore.

She'd gone soft in the heart. But not in the head. She was as steady and dependable as any of my council, always giving me good information when I needed it.

I hoped that helpful streak continued through my next request.

Wanda came into the kitchen and sniffed the air. "Do I smell lasagna?"

I grinned. "You do. Mavis just ran out for some Italian

bread." I sliced into the carrot on the cutting board in front of me. "I'm in charge of the salad."

Wanda nodded thoughtfully. She plucked two pieces of carrot off the board and ate one, then "accidentally" dropped one in front of her little beggar buddy. "Oops."

I sighed. "You might as well stop pretending you don't feed him people food. I know you do."

She shrugged off my insinuation and stole a whole carrot.

"Hey!" I'd peeled three carrots for the salad, and she'd just stolen a third of my effort. I hated peeling carrots. No way did I want to peel another one. I nodded toward the counter where I'd left the peeler. "You're peeling the replacement."

"Sure." She bit off a piece of her carrot and gave it to Monty, offering me a smug grin.

I sighed. "He's going to be insufferable if we all spoil him," I told her.

"He's a warrior," she responded, heading for the refrigerator to grab another carrot. "He deserves some of the spoils too."

She wasn't wrong. My dog had saved my life a few times already. And the creatures he'd gone up against had been terrifying. He hadn't hesitated to jump in and try to protect me. I owed him big time.

"I need your help with something," I said, scraping the last of my sliced carrot into the salad bowl.

"What?" Wanda opened the trash can and stood over it, peeling in a perfect, practiced motion. She didn't even slice chunks off her fingers like I usually did.

I examined the peeler slices on my hands and frowned. Someone needed to come up with a peeler that worked better. Eyeing Wanda's perfect strokes, I had to admit that maybe I was the problem, not the peeler.

I wasn't the world's best cook. I didn't burn water or anything, but my technique was below average. I brewed a mean cup of coffee, dished up a perfect bagel with butter, cream cheese, and jelly, and could make a peanut butter and potato chip sandwich with the best of them. But Mavis's love of cooking and Bev's technical expertise in the kitchen had never rubbed off on me.

Besides, Mavis loved to cook. Who was I to deprive her of that?

I quickly filled Wanda in on what had been going on. By the end of my story, she was leaning against the counter, the peeler and carrot in her hands forgotten. "Demons? Really?"

"I'm afraid so."

She turned around and absently placed the peeler into the sink, rinsing the carrot and shaking off the excess water. Carrying it over to me, she sat down and watched as I cut it up.

I let her stew on the information I gave her. I'd learned that the teen needed to assess a situation completely before speaking to it.

"This woman who's missing, do you think she's been possessed?"

The knife slid off the carrot and got my finger before I could catch it. The pain didn't hit me at first. Not until the first drops of blood welled up. "Ouch! Swear, curse."

Wanda's lips twitched. She was amused by my chosen form of swear control.

Sucking the wounded finger, I asked around it. "Why are you asking me that?" It hadn't occurred to me that Mrs. Wolde might have wandered off because she was possessed.

It probably should have. That was a rookie mistake on my part.

Wanda shrugged. "It seems like a good possibility."

"You're right. It does." Then I remembered I'd asked Davis to hunt her down. If she was possessed, he wouldn't have a chance with her. She could kill him without even breaking a sweat. Fear blossomed in my belly, twisting like a knife. "Is there a way to know if somebody's possessed before they get violent?"

Wanda pursed her lips. "Not really. Until they start changing their hosts, they generally lay low to avoid notice. It's not like in the movies, where the host starts spewing pea soup and stuff."

"How have demons been stopped in the past?"

She shrugged. "Except for rare instances where a Hellmouth managed to take hold, demonkind have been largely contained. The available magical history on demons is sparse. It mostly focuses on the vortex. I don't know if that's because demons are so hard to kill or if it's because an open Hellmouth is so catastrophic."

Of course I'd find a problem without a documented solution. I was an overachiever that way. I thought about her words for a minute and then said, "Okay, let's look at this from another angle. You told us that the Lares who shut down the last vortex sealed it from inside."

Wanda nodded.

"What did he use to seal it?"

She frowned. "His staff, I guess. That's the only source of concentrated power a Lares has."

"So, he threw himself into the abyss, and what? Just blasted the ever-living...erm...stuffing out of it?" I decided I'd really chosen the wrong profession if I was going to give up swearing.

Wanda shrugged.

Biting back frustration, I kept moving forward. "What we know is that the vulnerable spot is too far below the surface to reach from outside the vortex."

"Yes."

"And, we can assume that our best option with the demons, unless we can come up with a way to kill them, would be to return them to the vortex."

Her expression turned thoughtful. "Maybe. But if we can't close it, they'll just keep popping back out, and we'll spend the rest of our lives playing a gigantic game of whack-a-demon."

I grinned at the visual. "Right. But what if we could wrap the demons in the type of energy that kills the vortex? Like a trojan horse?" It was a far-fetched idea, but something I'd come up with while trying to think outside the box.

Her mouth opened and she stared at me, her gaze intense as if she were lost in thought. Then, I noticed she wasn't blinking.

Too late, I realized she was starting to fade away.

I jumped to my feet, reaching for her, but there was nothing I could do. The curse was yanking her back. Too fast. She should have been able to stay with us for at least an hour. But then, she shouldn't have shown up in the morning either.

I made a note to speak to Bev and Mavis about their work on Wanda's spell. I was really starting to think that whatever they were doing was changing Wanda's curse in strange ways.

We needed to figure out if those changes were dangerous to the teen.

11

LET FAILURE PIERCE A GUARDIAN'S PRIDE

The kitchen was warm, bright with the new overhead lights Trish had installed for me, and filled with hungry people enjoying Mavis's gooey, cheesy lasagna and garlic bread. My salad went over big with the women and Niele, who seemed to prefer greens and carbs to meat.

Along with his moss undies, Niele was wearing his pretty flower vest, which not only smelled great but was bullet and knife resistant to boot. I'd thought about having him make me one of those. It would come in handy in my new career.

Maybe he had a demon-resistant version. Hmmm.

I carried my full plate over to Niele, who was standing by the steps leading to the mudroom, his plate overflowing with salad and bread. "How's your dinner?" I asked the big man.

His wide smile made his thick-featured face look almost handsome. "Delicious. Especially the salad."

I laughed. "Suck up."

Niele's laugh was deep and soft, his shoulders shaking beneath it.

"How were things in town today? Any demon sightings?" I was worried that Rome was about to be infested by demons, and I wasn't sure how to stop it. Or what to do if it happened.

"Rome was quiet." He frowned, invalidating his implication that all was well. "Except for the shifting of the earth deep below the surface," he added.

"Has that gotten worse?"

He frowned thoughtfully. "Worse? I don't think so. But it's already pretty bad. I nearly got lost traveling from my home to the church this morning. And I've been traveling that route for fifty years."

My eyes went wide. "Lost? How?"

"The tectonic plates are moving around. The geosphere is skewed."

That didn't sound good.

"How's Gren?" Luke asked a quietly brooding Ferral behind me. The advocate was standing in the corner near the refrigerator, eating lasagna and sporting a serious glower. I'd asked him about Gren as soon as he'd arrived, but all he'd said was that the protector would heal.

That assurance, such as it was, left a lot of room for interpretation and worry.

Ferral shook his head, his gaze sliding to me and then quickly away.

Panic speared my chest, and my pulse spiked. I walked over to join the two shifters. "Tell me about Gren," I said to Ferral, my tone brooking no argument.

"Madam Lares," Ferral began in his most arrogant tone. "Your focus needs to be on the problem at hand..."

"Tell. Me," I repeated between gritted teeth.

He sighed, placing his half-eaten dinner aside. “As I said before, he’s under the best care available in this lamentably unmagical place.”

I arched a brow. “Where is he? Who’s taking care of him? And how badly is he hurt?”

The advocate’s jaw gained a mulish aspect. “He is fine…”

I closed my eyes on a wave of dizziness, grabbing hold of the counter before I fell. Voices came at me as if from a distance, hollow sounds that were as meaningless at that moment as Ferral’s empty assurances.

Someone touched my shoulder and then jerked away with a hiss.

My body throbbed, my muscles tightening almost painfully. Heat climbed through my clenched form, making beads of sweat pop out on my upper lip and along my hairline.

Rage pulsed through me.

Without warning, energy blasted away from me with a force that slammed into Ferral, crushing his big body into the wall behind him. My eyes snapped open, and I clenched my fist in front of his unrelenting face. Despite the violence of my rage, he stared at me as if he were watching rain fall from the sky. His arms hung loosely at his sides. His muscles were as relaxed as his expression.

I slowly raised my fist and he slid up the wall, skimming upward until he hit the ceiling.

The voices that my mind had muted suddenly broke over me like a wave on the front edge of a hurricane, swamping me with a chaos of emotions.

With what felt like superhuman effort, I clenched down on the raging magic trying to escape my control. I pulled air into my lungs and eased it out again through barely parted lips. The rage began to ease, and I slowly allowed my fist to lower, bringing Ferral with it. When his big feet rested on the floor again, I sagged, my knees turning soft beneath me. "What..." I licked my lips, brushing my sleeve over my sweat-dampened face. "What just happened?"

To my surprise, Ferral was the one who answered my question, his tone neutral, as if I hadn't just tried to wash the wall with him. "You just reached the next level."

I dropped into the nearest chair and rubbed my hands over my face. The room was absolutely silent around me. I lifted my gaze and found them all staring. A soft chirp above my head made me glance toward the light fixture in the center of the kitchen.

The bat hung from the metal and glass fixture I'd had specially made to match the lights and fans in the rest of the house. Even the flying rodent was staring at me through its unnatural yellow eyes.

"Level?" Luke finally asked.

Ferral nodded, pushing away from the wall and striding over as if I hadn't just tried to kill him. He eased himself gracefully into a chair next to me at the table.

"Gaining a legacy requires the passage of four levels," the advocate explained. "Understanding, Acceptance, Outreach, and Response. Madam Lares had already passed Understanding and Acceptance. It appears she has just attained the Outreach stage."

I frowned. "Outreach makes me beat up my own people?"

"Only when they deserve it," somebody mumbled behind me. Soft snickering accompanied the statement. The bat chirped in apparent agreement.

Ignoring them, Ferral continued. "Outreach in this context is nothing like you are used to in the human realm. The legacy is seeking validation that you have fully embraced the first two levels. Outreach is all about expanding your legacy. The level inspires a passion for your heritage magic. Embracing this passion occurs in many ways. Adding to your trusted group, stepping up your training, expecting more from yourself and others. Rage and frustration are necessary factors of that expansion because the magic running through your veins reduces your ability to slough things off. It will make you impatient with those who seem to defy your needs."

I grimaced. "So, you're telling me I'm going to become a raging jerk?"

He shrugged. "Only for a while. You will grow accustomed to the magic in due course."

"And until then?" I asked, feeling as if I wanted to go hide in my room.

Ferral pushed to his feet. "In the meantime, let us focus as much of that rage on our enemies as possible."

Gong!

I jerked in instinctive alarm at the doorbell that sounded like a summons. Bev had installed it for me as a housewarming gift. I'd loved the chime at the time. It seemed fitting to have a doorbell that sounded like a church bell when one was living in an old church. But since realizing that my early warning system as a Lares involved an actual church bell in my belfry, the doorbell sometimes gave me pause.

"I'll get it," my sister said, striding quickly toward the front door. A moment later, Bev's voice was heading back our way, accompanied by a second voice I recognized.

Chief Marshal followed my sister into the room.

I smiled at him. "You're just in time for dinner."

He nodded, looking wearier than I'd ever seen him. "Thanks. But I'll just take some water, please."

Mavis got him a glass of water, motioned to the table where I was sitting, and proceeded to fill a plate for him anyway. She was a genuine food bully. She'd never met a victim she didn't try to feed. I loved that about her.

My gaze searched for Ferral and found an empty spot where he'd been sitting. The jerk had slithered away when I wasn't paying attention. He really didn't want to tell me about Gren. Ice climbed through my belly at the thought. Was Gren in danger and Ferral didn't want to admit it? Or was he already dead?

Stars burst in front of my eyes at the thought, and I had to take several deep breaths before the panic receded.

"Thank you for this," Davis said, giving Mavis a warm smile that seemed to linger longer than a plate full of lasagna and salad warranted. "It smells delicious."

To my delighted surprise, Mavis's cheeks colored. "You're very welcome, Chief."

I let the man eat for a few minutes before I asked him for a report on his demon-possessed prisoners.

Conversation returned to normal as everyone returned to their meals. I let the sounds soak into me, enjoying the warm spot they created in my belly. A warmth that helped me temporarily set aside the icy fear I had for Gren.

When Davis set his fork down a few minutes later to take a drink of water, I asked, "Everything okay at the jail?"

He nodded, forking up some salad. "Those creatures you left to watch things..."

"The lost ones," Bev said, sitting down with us.

Davis nodded. "That's some level twelve nightmare stuff there, Aggy."

"Yes. But I trust my guy. If Ferral says they're safe, then they're safe." Even though he was a curse, swear curse pain in my backside.

Davis chewed thoughtfully for a beat and then swallowed. “They’re powerful creatures,” he admitted. “The Thomas’s don’t have a chance of escaping my jail with those two in the room.”

I winced at his use of the couple’s name. That was when I realized I’d already started to think of them as the demons they were possessed with. Their humanity was already fading away in my mind. That realization made me sad. “That’s one less thing to worry about then,” I murmured.

“If you don’t mind my asking,” Davis said. “What’s the plan? I can’t keep them in there indefinitely. Them or their nightmarish guards. Sooner or later, I’m gonna have to put a real prisoner in those cells.”

Sitting back in my chair, I scrubbed my hands over my face. A full belly and my recent power surge had drained my battery. Having been going at it since the wee hours of the morning wasn’t helping either. Weariness swamped me. I suddenly wanted nothing more than a nap.

The delicious scent of fresh-brewed coffee wafted beneath my nose, and Mavis placed a steaming black cup of vitality in front of me. “Thank you!” I told her. “You’re the best mom in the whole world.” Grinning, Mavis squeezed my shoulder. “You’re welcome, honey. Chief, would you like a cup?”

His answering grin was almost flirty. “Only if you’ll call me Davis.”

She tittered like a schoolgirl. “It’s a deal.”

I lowered my head to hide a grin.

Davis watched Mavis walk away, his gaze filled with appreciation.

I wasn’t sure how I felt about his interest in Mavis. I’d have to give that some thought once the world stopped ending. "As soon as I figure out how to draw the demons out of them, we'll give you your jail cell back, Chief."

"Any ideas on when that will be?"

"No. But we're working on it. I have a feeling we're pinched for time. Those demons are already creating changes in that young couple. The longer we let the nasty things keep control, the harder it will be to get them back."

I had no intentions of letting the demons win that battle. That young couple were my people. It was my duty to protect them. I hadn't done such a bang-up job of it so far. But I fully intended to step up my efforts.

I'd use every tool at my disposal.

12

A FRACTURED EARTH, A TREASURE FOUND

I'd fully planned to tackle some training with my magical staff after dinner the night before. But my body just wouldn't allow it to happen. I was dead on my feet. My weariness came much more from the emotional turmoil of the day than the physical.

At least, that was what I'd told myself.

One of the things I'd been trying to do since taking over the role of guardian for the town at the advanced age of forty-five was to get into better shape. Being a life-long couch potato promised to lend an element of resistance to that goal. But, to my delight, I'd discovered that it wasn't as hard as I'd expected. My body, always a little soft and overly padded, had tightened since I'd taken my magic. Some of the fat around my middle had melted away. Many, not all, of my wrinkles had smoothed out. Enough that I enjoyed looking at my face in the mirror again.

I didn't look like a twenty-five-year-old. But I felt strong and comfortable in my own skin in a way I hadn't for a very long time.

In pursuit of conditioning, I'd taken to running over the

grounds, including the magical woods behind the church, every morning. Since defeating the lost ones during my seating, I hadn't had anything attack me during my daily runs through the woods. However, I'd certainly enjoyed an array of magical creatures that both invigorated and entertained me as I ran.

Given my failed goal of practicing my staff with Trish after dinner, I'd decided to bring it with me on my run. I planned to find the perfect spot and perform some of the limbering moves Gren had shown me after I'd received the magical tool.

Monty, ever my stalwart companion, bounded happily across the grass ahead of me. Since Rome was easing toward fall, the morning air was cool and a light fog turned the grass into a fairy bog. The occasional flickering glow of magic flashed past just above the mist, the mystical auras of passing woodland creatures taking advantage of the fog's cloaking presence.

Despite the cooler season, the air was thick with the scent of Niele's flower gardens, which seemed to grow denser and spread further into the grass with every passing day.

The gnome did love his gardens.

I sighed happily, settling into my run with the long wooden staff clutched in my left hand. I'd been working on strengthening my left hand and arm so I could use both hands in battle.

The magical woods loomed ahead of me at the back of the property. I'd asked Gren and Niele, who'd both claimed to have traversed most of the wooded area, how big a piece of property it was. The Mystical Wood hadn't been laid out on the plot plan the realtor had given me when I bought the church, though my council members insisted it was mine.

Niele had shrugged at the question. Since he generally traveled beneath the ground, he had no visual cues to determine one section of earth from another. It was all just one big playground for him.

Gren, on the other hand, had experienced it from above as well as on foot. He could easily judge its size. But he'd simply shaken his head. "The woods are both unending and finite. They are not of this world, Aggy. Therefore they cannot be judged in that way."

Intellectually, his answer had been deeply unsatisfying. Physically, it felt accurate. As I moved from the grass of my oversized yard and stepped into the Mystical Wood, I felt the magic pinging along my nerve endings. The power filled my nostrils and coated my tongue, a mixture of verdant things and spicy cinnamon magic.

The leafy umbrella folded over me, the wood's embrace a welcome warmth in the center of my chest. Monty bounced into the air, tongue lolling and tail frantically whipping as a pixie flashed past just over his head, darting around the little dog to tease and tantalize.

He barked as the tiny creature flitted away, leaving quiet giggles in its wake.

Butterflies as big as my palm drifted into the air from a hundred different spots, their colors too vibrant to be real. They fluttered around me, the cumulative effect of their large wings creating a soft draft that tingled against my skin.

I stood with my arms out to my sides and closed my eyes, allowing the butterfly kisses to immerse me in delicate energy.

It was a favorite part of my day. For just a beat in time, I forgot the hellish vortex, the dangerously possessed citizens, the terrifying energy that kept Shadee and Molly in its thrall.

I let the gentle call of the butterflies invigorate me, refresh my soul, and give me the strength and inclination to do what I needed to do.

Then, just as quickly as they arrived, the butterflies were gone. I opened my eyes and smiled at my dog, who'd found a tree filled with giggling pixies and was trying to leap into the air to catch them.

With a resigned sigh, I balanced my staff between my flat palms, took a deep breath, and started the elegant, dancelike movements designed to make me and my magical stick work together as one. The six-foot-long wooden staff had a twisted metal grip at its center and a pretty orb on one end. The wood was very hard and had a swirling mahogany grain that seemed to come alive under the gilded light of the crystal orb. The energy that came from the staff was golden, like my own, and hot enough to sear through almost anything when wielded by someone as unschooled as I was. I figured the weapon would be a valuable asset someday. But not until I learned how to use it on at least a basic level.

At the moment, it was just dangerous.

As my muscles warmed, I stepped up my movements, increasing the power behind each thrust, the velocity feeding each turn and crouch. A sheen of perspiration coated my face, and my breath started to come in rapid pants. But the dance took my mind, enfolding me in its magic even as a golden aura began to fill the space where I moved.

The orb pulsed in time with my heart, the gentle thrum of magic against my palms seeming timed to the rhythm of my breathing. The ground beneath my feet was pliant, meeting each footfall, every increasingly exuberant movement, and sending me into the next with the ease of an enchantment.

A smile curved my lips. My heart soared. My mind was enthralled by the magic of the dance. I was so caught up in it all, I thought nothing of my first stumble, simply taking it in stride and sending the dance in a different direction. But, a moment later, the earth shuddered, and I stumbled again, nearly falling onto my face in the fragrant dirt.

A cry went up in the woods.

My head shot up.

The pixies shot into the air. A chorus of new sounds sifted through the otherwise quiet morning, bursting with apprehension.

Monty ran over to me, uncharacteristically frantic. He nipped at my feet, his tail set high and whipping the air.

His alarm infected me. I tried to assess the danger, my chest heaving from exertion, as the delicate balance of the Mystical Wood exploded into chaos around me.

Beneath it all, a deep rumble was growing. Like the growl of an enormous predatory creature, the woods roared and rumbled, the trees quaking beneath its snarl.

Then I stumbled sideways, my shoe catching the tip of Monty's paw.

My little hero yelped but kept nipping at my feet, more frantic than I'd ever seen him. I realized he was trying to get me to move.

"Ow! Monty, stop it."

I stepped away from his attempts to spur me, but he didn't stop. He renewed his nipping and, if it was possible, became even more agitated.

Without warning, the ground exploded upward, sending dirt and the fresh scent of torn vegetation into the air. Monty yelped again, his small body slamming into me as the ground split apart with a violence that took my breath away. I snatched him from the precipice and stumbled backward before the fissure could swallow us both whole.

Monty struggled out of my grip and ran toward home, stopping every few feet to bark back at me.

I started to run, but then I heard something that dragged my feet to a stop.

It was a distant cry, filled with the tension of pain and fear.

Somebody, or something, was in trouble.

"Go home!" I screamed to Monty. Then, ignoring the roar of the splitting earth, I grabbed my staff by its center grip and took off running toward the sound.

Thin fractures began shooting toward me from the main fissure, widening almost as quickly as I could step or jump over them. Behind me, Monty barked. I skidded to a stop when I realized he was following me over the fracturing ground.

"Come here, buddy," I called over the roaring of the earth.

He listened to me that time, tail drooping and eyes wide. Scooping him up, I started to run again.

The terrified cries I'd heard were lost beneath the clamor.

I ran as fast as I could, one eye on the growing split in the earth and one scoping out a pathway for me to run. Monty bounced against my chest. He quaked against me, clearly terrified of what was happening around us.

A crashing sound brought my head up, and I barely managed to dive behind a tree as several deer flew past, coming from the other direction. Wild-eyed and panicking, they'd have trampled us without even noticing they'd done it.

One deer, a female, stopped a few feet away from the

tree where we hid and turned back, the white underside of her tail bright in the dusty gloom of the imploding woods as she whipped it around.

She lifted her head and called out, then spun in a circle and began to pace.

With sudden clarity, I knew why. I stepped around the tree.

The deer jolted in fear, its liquid brown eyes going wide.

"Show me," I said in a quiet voice. She shouldn't have been able to hear me, but somehow she did. More than that, she understood. With a final whip of her tail, the doe spun again and took off running, her big body fast and agile between the trees.

I somehow managed to keep up, even with a wriggling Monty in my arms. By the time the doe skidded to a stop at the edge of the still-growing split, I was panting, my chest heaving from the effort. I settled Monty to the ground. "Stay close, little man."

As if he understood, he pressed against my calves, shivering with apprehension.

The doe snorted and bellowed again. I approached with caution, taking care to stay away from her deadly back hooves. Stopping beside the fissure, I gasped, my heart clenching with alarm.

Down at the bottom of the quickly growing break in the ground, two tiny fawns huddled together, bleating their fear. Even standing almost directly above them, I could barely hear the sound.

The mother shifted, dipping her head and kicking one back leg out with terrified frustration.

"I'll get them," I promised her.

She snorted and shifted forward, looking as if she was going to leap down into the fractured earth and join them.

"No," I told her, earning myself another aggressive snort at the tone in my voice. I forced myself to calm. "Let me?"

She stared into my eyes, her wet, brown gaze like a mirror into her troubled soul. Then she shifted sideways a step, snorted again, and bellowed to her trapped babies.

That was as close to agreement as I was going to get.

I pulled air into my lungs and tried to calm my racing pulse. It was nearly impossible to think when I was so amped up. But I had to save the two fawns. I didn't know how I knew that. But I did.

I lifted my staff and looked down on their frightened little faces. I could do it. I *had* to do it. I thought about what I wanted and reached for the energy frothing at my core. It was hot, agitated energy. Not what I wanted at all. But I didn't know how to cool it. And I knew I was running out of time.

The earth roared again, and the fissure jolted outward, nearly dumping the doe into the widening fracture with her babies as the ground was yanked from beneath one front hoof. Somehow she managed not to fall, dancing backward and spinning from the left to the right as her babies' cries grew more agitated.

When I looked at them again, they were at least two feet farther away.

Not good. The fracture was getting deeper as it grew wider. At some point, the babies would be lost.

I shook my head, determined that was not going to happen.

Lifting the staff to eye level, I focused on the orb, which had begun to glow under my determined push of energy, and thought about what I needed it to do.

I pointed the orb toward the twin baby deer and said, as calmly as I could, "*Leva*!"

The magic lashed out, hot and wild, and wrapped around the babies at the bottom of the split. They screamed in fear and tried to scrabble away, but their tiny hooves caught in the cracks and their wobbly legs weren't up to the task of saving them.

The mother reared back on a bellow, her front hooves slashing the air inches away from my head.

I yelped, ducking away. Closing my eyes, I took several deep breaths and willed my mind to calm. Slowly, I filtered out the chaos around me and set my focus on easing the energy into a gentle lift rather than a yank and a wrench.

The babies slowly started to float upward. They were still bleating with fear, but the energy held them in a gentle grip and was moving them in the right direction.

The mother's agitation didn't soften, but she stopped trying to kick me into the fissure, so I counted that as a win. As the twin fawns rose above the edge of the split, I blinked, realizing I had a new problem. They were too far away for me to grab.

I reached out with the staff and barely managed to touch one of them. The second baby had drifted toward the opposite side. If it landed over there, we'd have a new problem.

"Curse, curse, swear!" I said into the deafening sounds of breaking earth.

The mother trotted toward me, her gaze locked on her floating babies.

In desperation, I lowered the staff to the ground and extended my hands, easing two golden threads of energy from my fingertips. "Come, and be safe," I said, as loudly as I could so the command would rise above the sounds of the earth breaking.

The threads spider-webbed through the air, cutting the

distance between me and the fawns, and then wrapped them in a gentle hug of magic.

With a relieved sigh, I gave the threads a soft tug, carrying the babies toward the firm earth and out of danger.

The mother trotted over, dropped her head toward her babies, and gently nudged them.

I watched the little family, completely charmed as the babies struggled to their feet and wobbled closer to their mother.

She nudged them farther from the split and, with a final flash of her tail, started off through the woods, away from danger. The two babies scampered along after her. When they were twenty feet away from me, one fawn stopped and turned back, a silver aura sparking over its tiny body, and then hurried to join its family.

I sighed. "That was amazing," I told Monty. "And terrifying as *curse*."

He barked, his tail still whipping manically. Then turned his long nose toward the fissure as if to say, "Can we do something about that before it eats everything in sight?"

"Yeah," I said, sighing. "I'll see if I can fix it."

13

PAST MISTAKES AN ALLY BOUND

The earth rumbled beneath my feet. It caught me off guard as the plates shifted again, the fracture surging wider. A tree close to the new edge wavered violently, its roots dangling like skeletal fingers into the breach.

With a jolt, I saw my staff wobble on the edge, a single heartbeat away from falling inside. I started forward, only to be thrown off my feet again. The staff started to tip downward. Before I could climb to my feet, it disappeared over the edge.

"No!" Without a thought, I threw out a hand and sent a magical thread toward my staff. I shoved to my feet and ran, covering the distance to the edge of the breach in three, long strides. I arrived just in time to see my energy snag the quickly plummeting staff.

Relief swamped me as I yanked it upward. It hit my palm with a firm smack just as the world exploded around me.

I was out of time.

The fissure sliced into the remaining ground, brutally yanking trees out of the earth and sending boulder-sized rocks skyward. Roots of all sizes dangled like veins into the breach, bleeding rich black earth. I jumped aside, snagging Monty as a massive rock slammed down in the exact spot where we'd been.

That was the final straw.

With a rage-filled growl, I lifted the staff and pointed it at the fissure, screaming a command into the sustained howl of the dying earth. "Repair!"

Golden energy washed over the fissure, painting its irregular sides in magic that sizzled on the surface for a beat and then sank beneath the soil.

The fracture sent up another roar. Massive trees flew through the air like giant missiles, slamming into the boulder Monty and I had taken refuge behind. I sent energy above our heads, a protective bubble that shuddered and hissed as the fracture tried to smash us with its mammoth projectiles.

The earth shuddered hard. A manic wind tore past, deadly shards of wood and rock pitting my quickly erected protection. The ground convulsed again. The boulder at our backs fractured, the two pieces of it falling away. A tree slammed down mere inches from where I crouched, covering Monty with my shivering body.

A final gust of wind flung more debris in our direction.

I cried out as my nerves reached their breaking point, muddy tears sliding down my cheeks. I'd failed. The world was ending. And I didn't even know why.

And then, with a final gust of air that sounded like an enormous sigh, the woods was silenced.

I dared a glance toward the unnatural fracture in the ground and gasped. Shock sent me backward and I landed on my butt, staring open-mouthed at the ground.

The fissure was gone. I pushed to my feet and hurried

over, seeing a long, slightly raised line running the length of the once-broken space as far as the eye could see.

Like the healed remains of a horrible wound.

"Holy..." I slammed my lips closed as something moved out of the trees, gazes locked on me.

The two tiny fawns looked as if they'd aged several months since I last saw them. They stood and walked gracefully. Their sleek forms no longer showed signs of the silvery spots they'd had mere moments before.

But it was their eyes that caught my attention and held it. They sparked with silver light. One of the two had the beginnings of silver antlers jutting from its elegant head.

A moment passed. Then another. We were caught in in a moment of suspended animation fraught with awe and expectation. Finally, breaking the spell we'd been locked in, the two fawns inclined their heads, silver eyes sparkling like midnight stars, and took off bucking joyfully through the woods.

Tears rolled off my chin and splashed to the ground. I sniffed, scrubbing at the moisture running freely down my cheeks.

Monty barked. I looked down to find him wagging his tail, giving me his, I'm hungry, face. I laughed. Nothing got in the way of a dachshund's appetite, I reminded myself.

Not even coming within inches of being swallowed by the earth.

Sniffling, I expelled a long, harsh breath and turned my weary self toward home. "Okay, let's go get your second breakfast, little hobbit. Then I need to see how things are going at Golden Years and check in at the jail."

The mere thought of those two tasks made me want to start crying all over again.

I WAS in the shower when Monty started barking. I stuck my head out and listened, hearing the familiar voice of my magical historian. "I'll be out in a few," I called out to Wanda. I didn't get a response. But I hadn't really expected one.

Fifteen minutes later, I found her handing Monty a dog cookie he didn't need. Her own cookie, the human kind, was clutched in her other hand.

"Hey," I said, giving the teen a one-armed hug. "You're early." By about seven hours, but who was watching the clock? Besides me.

Wanda shrugged and crammed the last bite of cookie into her mouth.

"You want milk?"

She nodded, her gaze on the narrow door that led to the belfry. She and my resident bat had some kind of weird attachment for each other. Or, at least, she seemed attached to the bat. I had no idea what the flying rodent was thinking at any given moment.

I handed her a glass of milk while thinking about the bat. "I should name the flying rodent," I said out loud, surprising myself.

She looked at me over the rim of her glass. "You know she already has a name, right?"

I blinked. Clearly, I hadn't known that. I opened my mouth to ask what it was and got distracted by a soft weight against my leg.

"Meow."

I glanced down at Wraith. The feline had given me a drive-by rub and was winding herself around Wanda's ankles, oblivious to the grimace the girl threw her way.

Wanda apparently didn't care for cats. I plucked Wraith off the ground before she could escape me, burying my face in her soft, glossy fur. "Hello, girl. How are you today?"

Wraith batted at a strand of my shoulder-length black hair, seemingly captivated by the silver tips. Lately, I'd been toying with the idea of changing the color but hadn't done more than think about it. Given my current role and the company I was keeping, the straight black hair with silver tips seemed somehow appropriate.

"I have to leave," I told Wanda, watching her for signs of disappointment. I didn't fool myself into believing the girl cared about my presence one way or the other, but I felt bad leaving her behind anyway.

"Oh." She glanced toward the belfry door again. "Okay."

"I..." the words died on my lips as she turned those dark-as-night, overly made-up eyes in my direction. Then, I decided to go for it. "I don't suppose you want to come with me?"

She blinked in surprise. "Come with you?"

I smiled, happy she hadn't immediately shot me down. "Yeah. I need to check on some demons. I know that's not exactly a day at the shopping mall, but..."

Something that looked like real regret passed over her features. "I...can't."

I must have looked disappointed because she clarified. "The curse."

"Right. The curse." I set the cat onto the floor, where her fur rippled as if trying to expel my cooties. "Have you tried leaving since Bev and Mavis started working on getting rid of the hex?"

Wanda shrugged, her gaze following Wraith across the room to her bowls. "No. I assumed nothing had changed."

"We should give it a try," I told her. "What do we have to lose?"

She seemed to give it serious thought before speaking. Finally, she nodded. "Okay. Let's try it."

"Good!" I grinned. Then I frowned. "Wait. What *do* we have to lose? I mean... What will happen if it backfires on us?"

"I think I'll just pop back here."

"Okay. We can work with that, right?"

"Whatever," Wanda said. Though the look on her narrow face held a note of fragility in it. I hoped I hadn't created a situation where she'd be hurt even more by the curse. Suddenly, I had doubts. The last thing I wanted was to harm her...

"Come on," Wanda said, looping her arm through mine. "Don't overthink it."

"Right," I said. "I won't do that." But as we headed outside a moment later, I found myself holding my breath.

We stood on my small front porch for a moment after leaving the house, waiting for the curse to yank her back like a large, amorphous rubber band.

It didn't.

We stepped down off the porch and started toward the parking lot where I kept my elderly Range Rover. We stopped at the edge of the lot.

Nothing.

Wanda and I looked at each other and shared a smile. I gave her arm a squeeze beneath my own. "Looks like you're going demon hunting with me."

The pleasure and excitement in her dark brown gaze made my heart sing.

We climbed into my car, and I headed toward Rome. The small, picturesque town was only a couple of miles of gravel road away from my home. That couple of miles was far enough outside of town that it felt like I lived in the country, a feeling I loved, but still close enough to shopping and my friends to make it the perfect location.

Wanda fiddled with the radio. “I’m surprised you didn’t bring the little tyrant with you.”

I glanced at her, unsure at first who she meant. “Ferral?”

She laughed, settling on a song that sounded more like hand-to-hand combat than music. “He’s the *big* tyrant. I meant Monty.”

“Ah.” I chuckled. “The little man had a rough morning. I thought he should sit this one out.”

Her dark eyes widened. “Do you think this is going to be dangerous?”

We entered Rome and I drove slowly along Main Street, glancing around for signs of my team. They’d been taking turns keeping an eye on the town and the senior home since the night before. I spotted Niele lounging against the wall of the local hardware store, his mossy diaper pants and flowery vest looking extremely strange in that context. I frowned.

“What?” Wanda asked.

I shook my head. “I’m just surprised nobody makes fun of his outfit.”

“They’re probably relieved he’s not naked,” she said matter-of-factly.

It was my turn to go all wide-eyed. “He’s come into town naked before?”

Wanda shrugged. “He’d have had to, right? Before you showed up, the world was his naked playground.”

“Goddess in a girdle,” I muttered.

Wanda laughed. “You never noticed him, though, did you? Before you accepted the legacy?”

“No.” I frowned. “And I’ve spent a lot of time at that

hardware store too." Since the place also doubled as our only garden center, Niele had to have been in there a lot.

"That's because non-magic people don't see him the way magic people do."

"They see him dressed?" My expression must have shown my surprise because she giggled.

"Not exactly. They basically just don't..." Wanda frowned. "...see him. At all."

"Oh." There was something sad about that. "And magical people?"

"We see all the dangly bits." She snorted.

"Ugh!"

"But he's a gnome," she said, as if that explained it all.

I supposed it did. I was apparently the only magical person who hadn't understood that gnomes were nudity enthusiasts.

Two miles outside Rome on the opposite end of town from where I lived, the senior home loomed between a cornfield and a soybean field. The place looked quiet and empty in the late-morning sunshine.

The pseudo music changed again to something I would have classified as hard rock. I turned into the lot and parked, relieved when I turned the key, and the horrible shrieking on the radio stopped. "Okay. Here we are. Now when we get inside, I want you to stay cl..." The words died on my lips as I turned to Wanda and found only an empty seat.

She was gone. The spell had snatched her back.

Curse, curse, swear.

14

SEEN THROUGH A FAITHFUL ALLY'S EYES

I punched in the code on the front door and pulled it open, hesitating. The lobby beyond the glass entryway was darker than the last time I'd been there. The small lamp near the couch had been turned off.

I tried to remember if either Trish or I had turned it off. I didn't think we had. Alarm bells clanged in my head. It wasn't my Lares early warning system. Just normal, human alarm.

As I stood there wondering whether I should call for backup, the soft fluttering of wings sounded behind me. I whipped around, nerves already frayed, and watched a huge, black raven land on my car.

I stared at it for a moment, my heart thundering in my chest. The big, midnight-colored bird danced on the hood of my car, lifting its wings and cocking its head. "You should warn a girl before you sneak up on her," I told the bird.

The raven lifted its wings again and said, "Pee?"

The single word, delivered in the bird's scratchy voice with a questioning lilt on the end, made me laugh, reducing my tension by half. "Yes. You nearly made me pee my pants. Why are you here?"

The bird danced again, wings fluttering, and I realized it was mimicking my pee dance from the first time we'd met. I shook my head. "All right. You're here to make fun of me. I get it. I guess it's a slow day in bird world?"

The raven clacked its beak and lifted into the air, flying directly toward my head. "Ah!" I ducked as he flew over me, into the entryway, and slammed right into the interior glass, sliding bonelessly to the tile.

"Oh!" I exclaimed, hurrying over to make sure the raven was all right.

"Great," he told me in his husky voice. Then he fluttered his wings and hopped back to his feet to begin pecking at the glass.

"Yeah, that *wasn't* great," I sighed. "You scared a year from my life with that little maneuver." At that moment, I decided to call the odd creature Ray because it was easier than thinking about whether it was a boy or a girl bird.

"Life!" Ray exclaimed.

Sighing, I punched in the code for the interior door and pulled it open.

Ray ambled through the door, head on a swivel and feathers twitching.

"I guess you're coming with me," I said.

"Pee!" he squawked.

And that was that. Ray was either telling me he had to use the restroom, or he was there to keep me from peeing myself in fear. I was pretty sure it wasn't the former, and I'd spent enough time at the place since the vortex moved in to know he wasn't going to be able to accomplish the latter. So...

"What do you know about vortexes?" I asked Ray.

He waddled forward, head still on a swivel.

"Alrighty then."

Goochy Goochy Goo, Your Mom Needs you. Goochy Goochy Go, She Won't Take No!

Goochy Goochy Gum, You Know You Can't Run. Goochy Goochy Glee, You Know You Can't Flee.

I stabbed the button to answer Mavis's call. "Hey, Mom. What's up?"

There was a brief, startled silence. Then, "What's up? Are you kidding me? Where are you?"

"Ray and I are at Golden Years."

"Who's Ray? And why is he at the senior home with you? And, more importantly, who's there to back you up?"

"Ray's the raven, and your guess is as good as mine why he's here. I only know he was pretty determined to get inside." I grimaced at the memory of him hitting the glass.

"Okay."

"Apparently, Ray's my backup."

"Honey, you know that isn't safe. Wait for me. I'll be there in five minutes."

"Mom..."

"Don't you dare go into that courtyard without me, you hear?"

I sighed. "Okay. Ray and I will wait for you in the lobby."

"Promise me."

I heard a car door slamming. "I promise. What's going on at the jail?"

"I'll fill you in when I get there."

I disconnected and headed for the couch. "We might as well make ourselves comfortable," I told Ray.

Standing on the oval-shaped coffee table covered in old magazines, the big bird went perfectly still, staring at the couch. "What's up, Ray?"

He lifted his wings and danced sideways. "Great."

Something about the way he said it made me look where his beady black eyes were focused. I sucked air and stumbled backward on a sharp scream of fear.

"Ah!"

In the low light, I hadn't even seen the tiny figure on the couch until Ray drew my attention to her. She was so small she was all but swallowed up by the tall-backed couch. The elderly woman didn't react to either the raven or my obvious surprise. It took my brain a minute to catch up before I realized who I was looking at. "Mrs. Wolde?"

The woman lifted her head, her eyes dark pools in the shadowy light. Her small face, wizened and pale, held a soft smile. "Hello. Have you come to take me to my hair appointment?"

I sat down next to her. On an impulse, I took one of her pale hands, finding it unnaturally warm. "Are you feeling all right?"

The woman blinked and then nodded. "Yes, dear. Why do you ask?"

"We've been looking for you. Where have you been?"

"I've been in my room, of course."

The soft sting of her outrage almost made me smile. We'd looked in her room more than once. Had we looked under the bed? In the closet? The vacant look in her eyes told me it wouldn't have been unnatural, especially if she'd been frightened by the vortex's treacherous song, for her to have hidden.

I made a mental note to ask Trish how well she'd searched the room.

I gave the warm hand inside mine a squeeze. "I'm sure you're hungry?"

She shook her head. "I could use some tea, though, dear."

"Tea. Of course. I just need to do a quick check, and then I'll take you for some tea." I could drop her at the Sunflower Ranch after I got her the tea. "Can you sit here for a few minutes? I'll be right back for you. I promise."

Mrs. Wolde nodded and extracted her hand from mine, patting my knee. "I'll be right here."

I stood up. "Don't move, okay?" The last thing I needed was for the elderly woman to wander off again. It was a miracle she hadn't wandered into the courtyard and fallen into the vortex. I stared at her for a moment and then glanced at the raven. His sleek black head whipped from side to side. For a moment, I thought he was shaking his head no.

"Great!" he exclaimed, the single word too loud in the otherwise silent room.

Mrs. Wolde didn't twitch or react in any way to Ray's boisterous response. She was very calm. Much calmer than I'd be in her situation. I suspected she was suffering from some kind of cognitive decline.

"Okay. Stay here," I warned again. "I'll be right back."

Mrs. Wolde's gaze had found Ray, and she was smiling at him. Ray twitched and danced under her perusal. As I started toward the courtyard door, he lifted off the table and settled himself on my shoulder. His claws dug into my flesh for a beat and then relaxed.

It was clear the bird had been discombobulated by the elderly woman. I couldn't help wondering what it was about her that upset him.

I pushed through the glass door leading to the central common area outside and jolted to a stop. My pulse spiked, and I suddenly found it hard to breathe. The vortex had spread since I'd last seen it. The edges nudged up against the brick walls in a few spots, a smoggy haze rising from the places where it touched. Was it disintegrating the brick?

I struggled to breathe through a wave of sudden panic.

Goochy Goochy Goo, Your Mom Needs you. Goochy Goochy Go, She Won't Take...

I punched the answer button on my phone. I'd forgotten Mavis again. "Hey, mom. Are you here?"

"I'm at the outside the door. What's the code?"

I gave it to her and then gave her the code for the interior door. "I'm in the courtyard," I said. "It's not good, Mom."

Mavis sighed her disgust that I hadn't listened to her. "Be there in thirty seconds."

Ray and I were staring at poor Shadee when Mavis pushed the door open and joined us.

She frowned. "Goddess, she's a shadow of herself."

Mavis was right. Shadee looked to be little more than skin and bones beneath her tattered clothing. Where I could see it beneath the hood of her robe, her hair was singed into stubs on her head. Her fingers were charred too, blackened and bloody. I was suddenly glad I couldn't see her face. "This is horrible. We need to help her." As I said the words, I realized we didn't even know if Shadee was still alive.

As if reading my mind, Mavis said, "She's alive, honey. Or there'd be no point in her still being suspended there. The vortex would simply claim her."

I wasn't sure if I was happy she still lived under those tortuous conditions. It would almost be a mercy if she didn't.

My cell phone rang again, and I looked at the screen. "Bev," I told Mavis. "Hey?" I said as I answered the phone.

"Where are you?" my sister asked.

"Mom and I are checking in on Shadee." I started to tell

her I'd found Mrs. Wolde, but she cut me off. "We have a situation," she said.

My muscles stiffened with dread. "What's happened?"

"Molly Stanton has gone missing."

I threw Mavis a look. She frowned. "From the hospital? How is that possible? Don't they have some kind of security?"

"They're not equipped to keep people in, Aggy. But we checked the video feed outside her room, and it looks like she just climbed out of her bed and walked to the elevator."

I scrubbed a hand over my face. "Okay. Any idea where I should look for her?"

"No. But maybe she's coming back to Golden Years?"

That seemed logical. The facility was the only home Molly had known for almost a decade. "We'll hang here for a while then. Let me know if you find her in the meantime."

"Okay. Have you spoken to Ferral?"

I frowned. "No. He seems to be avoiding me. Any idea why?"

Silence met my question. Fear climbed up my fine with sharp fingers. "What?"

"I think it's about Gren."

My head was shaking before I realized it. Tears slid down my cheeks. I must have looked like I was going to collapse because Mavis put a surprisingly strong arm around my waist and eased me onto a bench. "Is he..." I swallowed hard, everything inside me wanting to rebel against the idea of what I was thinking. "I need to know if he's...dead." Stars burst before my eyes, and every muscle in my body turned to iron as I waited for her answer.

"I don't know any more than you do, Aggy," she said in a gentle voice. "The advocate isn't talking to anyone."

I lowered my head, scrubbing at my soggy cheeks. The

sharp stench of sulfur infused my senses, so thick on the air, I could taste it on the back of my tongue. "Okay. I'll deal with Ferral. Let me know as soon as Molly's found."

I disconnected without waiting for Bev's response and stared at Shadee. My chest felt as if it was filled with sand. My body felt heavier too. "I don't know what I'm doing," I thought.

As it turned out, I'd actually said the words out loud rather than thinking them.

"You're doing fine, honey," Mavis said. She dropped down next to me on the bench and wrapped an arm around my shoulders, pulling me close. I let my head rest on her capable shoulders as I had when I'd been a scared teen who'd just lost her mother and whose father had abandoned her. As it had then, Mavis's confidence in me helped to ease some of my self-doubt.

But, deep down, I knew I was a walking train wreck. Under my unskilled direction, everything was spiraling out of control. First the vortex, then the possessions, and now the missing woman and the mess in the woods, which I had no way to explain.

And Gren. Goddess help me if he died.

"That's enough!"

I jerked in surprise, my head coming off Mavis's shoulder. "What?"

Her pretty gray eyes snapped with anger. "I won't allow you to sit there and blame yourself for everything that's happened since this..." She swung an arm toward the boiling maelstrom. "...monstrosity appeared. None of this is your fault."

Had I been speaking my fears aloud again? "It *is* my fault, Mavis. I don't have a clue what I'm doing, and it's going to get everyone around me killed."

"Do you really have such a low opinion of all of us?"

When I blinked at her, she patted herself on the chest. "Do you think I'm an idiot?"

"No, of course not..."

"Do you think your sister is stupid? Niele? Trish? Luke? The advocate? The protector?" She glanced toward the vortex, where I saw with alarm that Ray was flying around Shadee as if checking her out. "Do you think that bird is an idiot?"

I felt a grin tugging on my lips. "Well, actually..."

Mavis seemed to be fighting a grin too. "Okay, birdbrain, I'll give you that one."

I chuckled, feeling better already. "I think you're all amazing. I'm not blaming this on you, Mom. It's my mess."

"But, that's the same as calling us idiots, honey. We believe in you. If we believe a totally inept person can be Lares, then that makes us blithering morons."

I shook my head, the action making me feel a little dizzy. I closed my eyes and took a deep breath, releasing it slowly. I felt better. "You believe in me because you love me. That doesn't make you stupid. It makes you wonderful."

She barked out a harsh laugh. "You think you're the only one who has doubts? We all worry whether we're doing the right thing, Agnes. We're all a little uncomfortable with the lot we've chosen. That's why we need you to live up to our expectations. And..." She lifted a hand to stop me as I started to object. "Our expectations aren't that you fix everything and be perfect. It's that you give everything you have to fix things. That you take the lead and allow us to do our best in support of you. That you trust us to have your back. Nobody expects you to be perfect. But we do expect you to do everything within your power to stop these people from being killed. Sitting around feeling sorry for yourself helps nobody. Especially you."

I shook my head. "When you put it like that, I feel a *lot* better."

Hearing the sarcasm in my voice, Mavis punched me on the arm. It hurt. "Ow! Hey..."

My vision slipped sideways, dipped, and twirled. Dizziness swamped me, and I shot to my feet, nearly hitting the ground as vertigo made my head spin. I threw out an arm, and Mavis grabbed my hand, steadying me.

"What is it?" she asked, sounding alarmed. "What's happening?"

"I don't..." I blinked, rubbing my eyes as an image appeared behind my lids. For a moment, I thought I might throw up. But the feeling slipped away and the dizziness eased.

I found myself looking at a nightmare.

A nightmare whose lips started to move.

15

THE LARES MUST HER PEERS APPRISE

It took me a moment to realize I was looking at Shadee. Not all of her, though. I was looking into her face, from mere inches away, close enough to bring the stark horror in her brown gaze into terrifying focus.

Deep hollows, like bruises, filled her cheeks. The whites of her eyes were yellow, the skin around her eyes was burnt and blistered. Her eyebrows were singed. The tiny braids that used to surround the nurse's face were burned away, and pain was etched into every line in her face.

But her eyes...

I shuddered under their impact.

And when her dry, blistered lips opened, I tensed in dread of the words to come. "Madam Lares," Shadee said, her voice cracked and broken, "You must find her." Shadee swallowed hard, her throat convulsing as if the simple act was more painful than words. "You need to stop her before dis is done. Find her..."

"Who do I need to find?" I asked. "Who can stop this, Shadee? How can I help you?"

The horror-filled eyes closed, and she swallowed again.

As they reopened, I reached out, finding nothing within reach of physical touch. The only place I was close enough to help was in my mind's eye. And that was no help at all.

"Find her, Madam Lares. You must stop her before dis is all lost."

The world swung sideways again, unbalancing me and making my stomach roil. I leaned heavily on Mavis, who, thankfully, still clutched my hand.

As the picture in my mind slipped away, I forced my eyes to open. Riding out the quick burst of dizziness sliding through me, I took a deep breath and looked at Mavis.

Her pretty face was contorted in pain before she lowered her head, smoothing the expression away.

"What?" I looked down at her hand and gasped. Bruises already discolored her pale skin where I'd been clutching it. "Oh, Mavis! I'm so sorry."

She shook her head, putting the hand behind her back to keep it from me. "Tell me what you saw."

I winced, my gaze flying to Shadee. She still floated face down, arms outstretched and fingers curved downward. The fingers seemed more claw-like than before. From pain? Or just because her body was shriveling beneath the Hellmouth's effects.

Tears burned my eyes. "I saw Shadee's face. She spoke to me."

Mavis frowned. "What do you mean you saw her face?"

"I don't know, I just...it was just there."

"How?" Mavis asked. "Is this some new guardian power?"

I shook my head. "I think I was seeing her through Ray's eyes. It happened before when the locusts struck Rome during my seating." That had been a mess which had taken every bit of my imagination and newly found magic to fix.

Mavis nodded. “He *was* flying around her when you went weird on me.”

I glanced toward the soft sound of flapping wings. The raven fluttered downward, landing on my shoulder with a heartfelt caw.

I winced at Ray’s loud cry mere inches from my ear. “Okay. That wasn’t necessary, was it?”

His response was to dance over my shoulder then flap his wings, smacking me in the cheek with his feathers.

Mavis chuckled. “Most people just get a canary and put it in a cage. You have to have a big old mouthy raven who screams inappropriate things and dances the pee dance on your shoulder.”

“Such is my life,” I said, sighing.

Mavis’s smile slid away. “So, what did she say?”

“That I need to find *her* and stop *her* before this is done.” I thought about that, realizing it could mean many things.

“Her who?”

“I wish I knew. Molly, maybe? She’s the only one who’s missing.”

Mavis nodded. “Shadee did say Molly was lost to the magic. Maybe she inadvertently triggered this, and she can stop it.” We stood in silence for a moment, staring at Shadee.

“Bev thought maybe Molly was heading this way.”

“What?” Mavis’s eyes went round. “I thought she was in the hospital.”

“Oh. Yeah. About that...”

A thunderous pounding came from the front of the building. It should have sounded muffled from that distance, but I could hear it as if I was standing near the door.

Not a good sign.

It was an even worse sign when I saw the lost princess standing in front of the entrance.

I stood on the other side of the glass, staring at her. She stared back, her exotically slanted, eyes alight with the usual fiery centers. Narrowing my gaze on the princess, I couldn't help thinking her eyes looked even more agitated than before.

Sliding my gaze away from Princess Layla, I checked out the five creatures arrayed around her. They all looked like a version of her, except that the males were at least two feet taller and had skin as black as night. Their eyes also weren't alight with fire, a feature that must be limited to the royal members of the race. The single female attendant had a thick halo of black hair as opposed to Layla's golden-blonde. The men had no hair at all.

"What do you want?" I asked, not even tempted to open the door.

"I need to speak with you, Lares," the creature said. The way she spoke my title told me we were probably never going to be friends.

"Why?" I asked.

Mavis came up beside me, energy spitting at her fingertips.

The princess smiled condescendingly. "You believe your pitiful magic will work against us?"

Like me, Mavis's gaze slid very deliberately over the five guards. She shrugged. "Maybe not, but we won't go down easily, demon."

I could feel the tension in the shoulder touching mine, but I was impressed. Mavis gave no indication of fear in her voice, expression, or demeanor. Once again, I was struck by the reality that my adopted mom was a serious hardbutt. Who could have guessed?

The princess rolled her fiery eyes. "We haven't come to attack you, foolish humans. I have come with information. Open the door and let us in."

"*You* can come inside," I told her. I nodded toward the guards. "They need to stay here, between the glass doors."

The princess eyed the glass and finally nodded. I was pretty sure they could just shatter it if they wanted to. That she hadn't done that...yet...told me she was trying to play nice for the moment.

I punched in the code for the outside door and retreated through the inside door, which Mavis held open until the princess was inside with us. Though she no longer had magic snapping at her fingertips, Mavis stepped back from the princess and started weaving a spell on the air.

I left her to it. "Come and look at the vortex." I turned my back on Layla and headed outside, counting on her to follow.

Once outside, the princess walked the perimeter as best she could. The buildings blocked the sides so she couldn't circle all the way around. Her gaze kept sliding to Shadee. "It is killing her."

I frowned. "I'm aware."

Her gaze whipped to mine. "Why haven't you saved her?"

I would have laughed if I didn't feel like crying. "I've been told it's not that easy."

The lost princess circled around to the other side and peered at the nurse, then the abyss. "I can help you extricate her."

Hope surged, but I shoved it brutally down. "Oh? Why would you do that?"

The princess strode back to me, her movements surprisingly graceful. "I wish to make an alliance with you."

I blinked, startled. An alliance with a powerful entity like the royal lost ones would be a real coup. For a town that was built at the epicenter of a magical vortex, they could prove very useful. "At the risk of repeating myself, why would you do that?"

Her smile made my stomach twist with alarm. All those teeth did not make me feel secure. I glanced toward the lobby, wondering why Mavis hadn't joined us. "You need help defeating these demons," she said. "And I need trusted allies in the human realm."

When I just stared at her, she clarified.

"As you can imagine, magical humans do not trust us. I understand why. Since their enemy is also my enemy, I can appreciate the fear they feel when they look at my people. Physically, we resemble their enemy. But in our hearts, our souls, we are not the same."

"Explain."

She looked down as if frustrated by my question. Twining her long fingers together, she shook her head. "Have you fully embraced your legacy, Madam Lares?"

I hadn't expected that question. It caught me off guard. "I..."

Her head came up, and the fire in her eyes flared with emotion. "You came to your seating completely untrained, blind even to magic and the magical world. You fought your way through the process, barely clinging, at times, to your sanity and your life. But you have the soul of a Lares, though I'm not sure you believe it still."

She was right about my doubts, and that made me uncomfortable. I tried not to admit my misgivings, even to myself.

"A determined soul is key in the magical world. Your heart, your passion, your soul lead you to protect your dominion. That is why you succeeded in your seating. That is what will make you successful as a Lares."

It hit me then. "You want to improve your image by attaching yourself to me."

She laughed, the sound a smoky growl. "I respect your directness. But do not worry, it won't be one-sided. You need my help, Lares. We both know this."

Again, she was right. "I agree. I believe an alliance with you is a good idea, Princess."

Her head came up, a smug expression on her demonic face.

"But, I don't fully trust you," I went on. "You need to prove to me that it is a good idea to ally with you."

"How do you propose I do that?"

My gaze slid to Shadee. "Help me save Shadee, and then fight alongside me to defeat any demons who come through this goddess-forsaken abyss."

She inclined her triangular, horned head. "Agreed."

"Human life is foremost. The possessed must be purged and saved, not killed."

"If it is possible, Lares, we will save them."

I stared at her for a moment, trying to judge her sincerity. Was she just telling me what I wanted to hear? "That will be central to any future alliance."

The lost princess inclined her head again. She didn't seem bothered by the condition I'd set.

"Good. Now, tell me how we save Shadee?"

Her fiery gaze slid toward the suspended woman. "It is both simpler and more complex than you might believe," she told me. I watched her move along the edge of the vortex. The shimmering surface bubbled like pudding wherever she moved, as if her mere presence was agitating it.

It probably was. Though they were of the demonic realm, lost ones were exempt from using the abyss. Demons had apparently made the earthly realm into their very own penal colony for indicted and ostracized demons. I wondered, briefly, what Layla had done to bring about the banishment of her people.

"I must bring two of my people inside."

Narrowing my gaze on her, I considered her demand. She stood with her perfectly manicured hands clasped in front of her, a neutral expression on her terrifying face.

I didn't like it. But I liked the idea of leaving Shadee suspended over the abyss even less. I nodded. "Two. No more."

She inclined her head in a shallow bow. "As you wish." With a flick of her hand, every door in between the courtyard and the entrance flew open. Mavis had been standing in front of the door to the courtyard, her hands cupped around a spell that hung in front of her in the air.

Her eyes going wide, she lifted her hands.

"Hold that thought, Mavis," I told her. "Allow two of her people through."

Mavis looked at me as if she thought I'd lost my mind but finally stepped back. Two of the lost ones strode past her like she wasn't even there and joined their princess beside the abyss.

The black and bloody liquid had bubbled higher when the princess neared it. When there were three of the lost ones standing near its edge, it began to churn even more violently. The three of them stood a distance away from me and conferred quietly near its edge. The liquid jumped and whirled, splashing over its edges as if intending to leap its bounds.

I stepped back, anxiety suddenly making it hard to breathe. "Princess, what's happening?"

"Is everything okay?" Mavis asked from the doorway. "Do you need me?"

The lost princess nodded at her people and walked toward me. "You should back up a bit. Just in case."

I felt my eyes go wide. "In case what?"

"Aggy?" The tension in Mavis's voice had me whipping my gaze toward the abyss. I turned just in time to see one of her people back up and start running, flinging himself into the air and...

"Goddess, no!"

The huge demon slammed into Shadee and wrapped himself around her just as they plunged into the boiling contents of the abyss.

Stunned silence followed the horrendous display. Then I started to scream, rage bringing sizzling energy to my fingertips. I took off running, fully intending to fling myself into the abyss in a no-doubt fruitless attempt to save Shadee.

Mavis screamed my name.

I ignored her, leaping into the air at the edge of the vortex and...finding myself jerked to a stop with a painful grunt as an iron band wrapped around my waist and yanked me away.

I'd been snagged right out of the air by Layla's second guard.

I screamed again, my rage hotter than the surface of the evil pool at my feet. The lost one was impossibly strong. Despite my enraged efforts to get free of his grip, he held me with seemingly little effort, carrying me back to Layla.

The princess barely spared me a glance. "Calm yourself, Lares. We are doing as you asked."

"I didn't ask you to fling her into the boiling pit from Hell!"

She rolled her eyes. Actually rolled her eyes. I'd thought I was enraged before, but her careless action literally stole the breath from my lungs.

If I could get to her, I'd kill her with my bare hands. But I couldn't get to her. The goddess-bedamned creature holding me was impervious to my attempts to escape its grip.

In sheer desperation, I slammed an energy-painted hand against the creature's throat and released everything I had.

He jerked, stumbling back a few steps, but was otherwise unfazed.

"Aggy, look out!" Mavis screamed.

My head shot up, my gaze sliding to the vortex, and I immediately wished I hadn't looked. "Curse!" I screamed as the liquid in the massive, stinky hole rose up like a wave in a tsunami, curling over itself and heading for unclaimed ground beyond the Hellpit's limits.

"Run!" I screamed, my legs kicking and elbows flying in an effort to escape the monster's hold.

Layla flipped a hand in my direction, and her minion released me without warning. I hit the ground hard, feeling the impact in my tailbone like a baseball bat applied to my backside. The boiling black liquid rolled over its boundaries and hit the grass, sizzling and flaring as it began eating its way in my direction.

I jumped to my feet and started to run, not waiting to see if it would stop.

The next wave was even higher. It hit the ground harder, splashing the blistering, poisonous liquid against the buildings and everything else in its path. The small pavilion in the center of the once-pretty courtyard collapsed beneath the liquid's blazing hunger, its wood and shingles melting away before my very eyes.

The wave of oily death slithered to a stop mere inches from the second guard's cloven hooves.

Tears slipped from my eyes. I'd failed Shadee. There was no way she could have survived that cauldron.

"Aggy, look!" Mavis said, grabbing my hand.

I reluctantly turned back to the vortex, just as something huge and black ejected from its center and flew through the air toward Layla and her minion.

The minion stepped up and lifted his arms, letting the slimy black projectile hit him in the chest.

I yanked energy into my fingertips and started forward. I was not allowing any more demons into my town. I'd kill whatever that was before it got its sea legs.

Mavis fell in beside me, energy spitting from her hands too. Between us, I figured we could at least slow the newcomer down so Layla's people could take care of it.

The black blob on the ground split into two.

I groaned internally. One we might be able to battle. Two was...really curse, curse unfortunate. "Get your people in here, Princess Layla," I told the royal lost.

She stepped forward. "That won't be necessary, Lares."

I narrowed my gaze on her. "I'm really not happy with you right now, *Princess*," I spat out. "You should probably just do as I ask."

She stared at me a moment, giving nothing away. Then she sighed. "You don't want to attack her, Madam Lares. She's already weak and infirm. You'd probably kill her."

"Her?" The first niggling of doubt made me turn back to the slimy creatures on the ground.

"Madam Lares?" a rusty voice asked.

My heartrate spiked. Even raspy with pain, I recognized that voice. "Shadee?"

Some of the oily black substance had slid off and seeped into the dirt around her, and I finally recognized the nurse's familiar face. Dropping to my knees next to her, I ran a hand over her filthy cheek. "Goddess, Shadee, I thought you were a goner."

She wheezed out a laugh, sounding like a wounded animal expelling its last breath. "That makes two of us," she agreed.

"I called for an ambulance," Mavis said. She knelt on Shadee's other side and took her hand. "You're going to be fine," Mavis said in a soothing voice. "Just try to rest."

Shadee shook her head. She closed her eyes and sighed. "I'm not ever going to be okay again," she murmured, so softly I wasn't sure I'd heard her right.

Layla touched my shoulder.

I surged to my feet, beyond angry.

The princess held up a hand. "You must not give in to histrionics, Madam Lares. There is much to do and little time to do it."

I wondered if she'd even feel it if I punched her right in the face. Probably not. And, I'd likely break my hand on her ugly mug. "What do you mean, we have very little time?"

Her gaze skated to the still roiling vortex. The liquid inside was agitated, definitely pushing the boundaries it had created for itself. But it was no longer flinging itself around what remained of the courtyard.

For the moment, the deadly mire was contained. A small victory.

"Removing the voodoo queen has stepped up our timeline," Princess Layla said in her smug voice.

"What do you mean?"

"I mean, that she was feeding it, yes, but she was also regulating its growth. As long as it had a nutrient source, it was content to linger, occasionally releasing a demonic soul into your world to prepare and await the moment it gains full power."

I barely retained a shudder. "And now?"

"And now, it will be forced to grow and gather new sources of energy, so it can create the permanent pathway between earth and the demon realm that it wants."

"Can you give us that in English, please?" Mavis asked.

Layla sighed, so put upon by us mere stupid humans. Her voice changed, sounding more like Wanda in her intonation and choice of words. "What I'm telling you ladies is that this b-eye-itch is about to blow. And we're going to be caught with our pants around our ankles if we don't get off our butts and prepare to kick its keister."

I looked at Mavis. She looked at me. "That seemed clear," I said.

She nodded. "Yep. Crystal."

16

WHEN MALEVOLENT FORCES SPREAD THEIR WINGS

"It would have been nice if you'd told us that before you ripped Shadee out of there," I told the lost princess.

She shrugged. "Would you have asked me to leave her there?"

Dangit! I'd walked right into that one. "No."

"Then...?"

I fought a lip curl, sighing. "Okay, so how much time do we have?"

"I have no idea."

I just stared at her, my fingers clenching of their own volition.

She stared back for a beat and then turned to the guy who'd snagged me away from the abyss when I'd been about to go in after Shadee. I owed him an apology for all the horrible things I'd been thinking about him at the time.

He caught me looking at him and smiled, the mountain range of jagged teeth nipping the apology right out of my brain.

"My guards will stay and monitor the vortex. They'll report any changes back to me."

I nodded. "I'll post someone here too."

"That won't be necessary," Layla said. She stared down her nose at me, which wasn't easy given that her "nose" consisted of a couple of slits. "If we are to be in an alliance, Madam Lares, you must trust me."

"No, I must not." My smile wasn't nice. I hadn't intended for it to be. "You must earn my trust. Until then, I'd prefer to trust but verify."

Flipping a hand at me, she glided toward the building, her strides loose and fast.

I looked at Mavis. "Stay with Shadee. I'll send the EMTs back to you when they get here."

Mavis nodded. "I'll do an obfuscation spell of the abyss and..." She flipped a hand toward the two lost ones. "Those."

I mentally berated myself. I should have thought of that. The EMTs would be human. They'd need new undies if they saw the demons and the bubbling vortex they were guarding.

I hurried to catch up to Layla. "You and I need to talk about what happened in there. I have an idea how we might be able to use that little trick against the vortex."

She shrugged, seeming more like the teen on my council every minute.

It didn't deter me. "How much do you know about the Hellmouth? About how it works? How to get rid of it?" I asked.

"It cannot be gotten rid of. The best you can hope for is to make it dormant."

I grimaced. That was not good news. "Ok, how do we do that?"

We entered the lobby, and I noticed the gloominess of the space. The air had smelled like rain earlier in the day. Clouds were likely building outside. I flipped a light switch, and nothing happened.

An icy wind slipped over me, bringing gooseflesh up along my arms. Someone had turned the air conditioning down. I headed for the thermostat on the wall and stared at it, confused.

"What is it?" Layla asked, looking over my shoulder.

"It's cold in here."

She glanced around, her slanted eyes narrowing. "Yes. It is."

"The thermostat is set at seventy-eight."

"You are correct," she said. "That is cold. Why does that concern you?"

Lifting my brows, I stared at her as if she'd lost her mind. "You think seventy-eight is cold?"

A shadow danced across the wall, the impression of a long snout filled with oversized teeth giving me a horrifying sense of déjà vu. "Oh. Oh."

"Oh, oh?" Layle's nostrils flared. She skimmed her gaze toward the wall where I was looking.

My nostrils pinched under the putrid scent blowing over us. "I don't like the looks of this," I told her.

"On that, you and I can agree," Layla said.

The shadow ripped from the wall and flew toward us, all teeth and claws and charcoal gray nothingness.

Without warning, Layla straight-armed me, planting a hand on my chest and shoving me into the back of the couch. I hit the rounded back and flipped cheeks over tea kettle onto the seat, landing with my knees on the floor and my face buried in the cushions.

The big piece of furniture slammed into my belly. I fell backward and looked up, my eyes going wide.

Layla was draped over the back of the couch, her claws raking at the shadow and her teeth bared. Blood glistened on her face, neck, and chest, and she seemed to be losing the battle with the thing attacking her.

I shoved to my feet and screamed. "Help her!"

Her people banged on the front door. I threw out a hand, and the door slammed open, hitting one of the lost ones in the chest and knocking him into the glass divider. The glass shattered beneath his weight. The guards poured into the lobby. I ran to the courtyard door, wrenching it open. "Mavis, stay out there. Protect her."

I didn't wait for a response. I spun around and lifted my hands, sending twin jolts of golden energy into the back of the shadow that was still brutalizing Layla.

The insubstantial-looking creature absorbed the energy without apparent notice and continued to rip at Layla.

Her people threw themselves into the fray, but the shadow sent them flying with a single swing of an arm. One collided with the receptionist's desk, turning it to kindling. Another hurtled through a round glass conference table across the room. The third bounced off an armchair and boomeranged back, claws out and fangs exposed. The female guard flew off the ground, wrapping herself around the shadow and ripping into its charcoal throat with her deadly-looking teeth.

The shadow reared up, finally leaving Layla, and spun around, trying to dislodge the lost one on its back.

I sent more magic into its body, firing narrow, focused jets of energy, like bullets, to increase the deadliness of my attack.

The female guard went flying, slamming into the glass

of the entry and shattering it into a billion tiny shards. She crumpled bonelessly to the ground, unmoving.

The shadow turned back to Layla. The lost princess also wasn't moving. And she was a bloody mess.

I swallowed hard. I couldn't let that thing finish her off. If it hadn't already.

Sucking air into my lungs, I wished with everything inside me that I'd brought my staff. If ever an uncontrolled blast of terrible power was needed...

The air blurred in front of me, something hit my palm. I looked down and felt my eyes go wide. It was my staff. But it was the size of a sword instead of a walking stick. The orb at the end was the size of a golf ball instead of a baseball.

The shadow roared and flew at me, its amorphous form wavery and hard to follow with the naked eye.

I didn't think. Didn't hesitate. I couldn't. There wasn't time. I snapped my arm up and then down, expending the staff to its full length, like a cop's billy clubb. Without hesitating, I slammed the orb into the center of the thing's chest, screaming with the effort of sending everything I had into my magical weapon.

The world erupted in light. It burst in a wave of heat and golden illumination that scoured across my skin like sandpaper over soft wood. Fire erupted around me, putrid and oily and hungry for blood. But the golden light caught the flames, ate them away, and forced the shadow into the light.

For the space of a single heartbeat, I saw it clearly, and immediately wished I hadn't.

The demon...because that was what it had to be...was long and stringy, with transparent skin that was a repulsive bluish yellow color, like spoiled milk. Its insides were visible through its skin, the shriveled shapes of its organs covered in seeping wounds and warty bumps. The thing had no skeleton that I could see, but its claws were as long as my fingers and it had teeth like an alligator, wrapped in an elongated snout.

Drool dripped from its open maw, and its pale, pink eyes wept from the burning force of my light. It ducked its head and screeched, the sound ripping into my ears like knives. Pain shot through my knees and I realized they'd given out, dropping me to the floor in the middle of a billion shards of glass.

The glass held the golden light of my energy, throwing it back in a deadly prism that had the demon stumbling backward, covering its filmy eyes with its clawed hands.

My thoughts turned muzzy. My bones felt like melted butter. The energy from my staff pulsed and wavered on its target.

I was clearly at the end of my resources. But I couldn't let that thing off the mat. I had to finish it. Except I wasn't going to last that long.

Gren, I thought, my mind battling against a cold, charcoal fog.

I wavered on my knees. Flinging out a hand, I was able to stay upright by grabbing hold of a wooden leg of the toppled couch. Gritting my teeth, I managed to send a fresh wave of power into the monstrosity in front of me.

But it didn't last long. My strength was giving out. The room around me turned fuzzy as weariness clouded my vision. My mind wavered, trying to shut down. I started to topple beneath the fog. As my head slammed into the glass-covered carpet, a soft, distant voice growled out, *I'm coming, Aggy. Hold on.*

But I couldn't hold on. I tried to get up again. My melted butter bones collapsed. I tried to form a thought...come up with a plan...but my thoughts scattered like butterflies under the predatory eye of a hawk.

I threw out a hand, but no magic emerged. I was done. Empty. Alone.

My lids fluttered closed. My thoughts swirled away. And the fog rolled over me.

THE WORLD WAS WITHOUT LIGHT. Sound came at me from the end of a long tunnel, muted and dull. There were shouts and screams and the chaotic sounds of things breaking.

One shrill scream rose above the rest, dragging me closer to the surface and waking the warning bells in my mind.

Gren?

A snarl. The sound of snapping teeth. And a snotty voice in my head. *Madam Lares! You have a job to do. Get off your tookus and do it!*

Not Gren. Curse, swear, curse.

I forced the fog from my brain. It relinquished its hold reluctantly, slowly. When my eyes finally opened, I scanned the room for signs of the demon. All I saw were Ferral, Mavis, and a black spot on the rug a few feet behind them. "Where is it?" My voice was as broken as I was, an almost indecipherable croak of sound.

Mavis hurried over and dropped to her knees, pulling me into a hug. "Thank the goddess, you're all right. We were starting to think you weren't going to wake up."

I hugged her back, relieved to have proven them wrong. "I'm fine. Just worn out. I threw everything I had at that...thing." My gaze lifted to Ferral's. "I called Gren. Why didn't he come?" I was getting sick of the advocate's refusal to answer my questions. He was going to answer me if I had to put a shock collar on his dog-shifter neck and give him a series of thousand-volt love taps.

He just stared at me, his lips curved in a smug smile. My fingers clenched around that imaginary collar.

"He's..." Mavis glanced at Ferral, and she frowned.

My heart started pounding out an SOS. I shoved to my feet, staring Ferral down. "Where is Gren, advocate. Tell me or I'll..."

"Aggy?"

The voice was soft, deeper than a well in the Sahara, and slightly rough. My gaze jerked away from the advocate and swung toward the delicious sound. Immediately, my entire body warmed, my pulse spiking from something entirely different than before. "Gren." His name came out of my mouth sounding like a caress, my tone nearly as husky as his had been. "You're okay."

He was standing in front of the shattered doors, his long body straight and whole. His brown gaze was filled with heat, like molten chocolate on the verge of boiling. "I am."

We stared at each other for a long moment, the air between us taut with unspoken emotion. I wanted to cut the distance between us and yank him against me...to wrap myself around him and hold on tight until my heart stopped pounding with fear that he'd been permanently broken somehow. I wanted to press my lips against the pulse I could see pounding in his throat and inhale his delectable scent.

But I didn't do any of those things. Instead, I smiled, saturating my gaze with the emotion as a promise for later. When we didn't have so many witnesses.

Right on cue, two EMTs came into the lobby with Shadee on a gurney between them. They looked unfazed, so

I knew that Mavis had put them under an obfuscation spell when they'd arrived.

I hurried over and the two men stopped the gurney. "How is she?" I asked, my hand seeking Shadee's arm and stopping when I saw the badly burned flesh.

"She was seriously hurt in the explosion," one EMT said, eyeing me. "Are you okay, ma'am? We have room for two in the ambulance."

I chuckled wearily. "I look that bad, huh?"

He struggled for a response until I rescued him. "I'm fine. Just get her to the hospital. If she wakes up, please tell her Aggy will be there to see her soon."

The EMT nodded. "Sure. You take care of yourself, ma'am. Being caught in an explosion is no small thing. Sometimes the damage doesn't show up right away. You really should go to the hospital and get checked out."

Rather than continue to argue, I nodded and thanked him. I waited until they'd loaded Shadee into the back of the ambulance and driven off, sirens blaring, before turning to Ferral. "Where's the princess?"

"She's been taken to a healer," he told me.

I nodded. "She was in bad shape."

"The lost ones have superior healing energies," Gren said, moving closer. He glanced toward the black spot on the carpet. "The shadow demon was in bad shape too when we arrived." His perfect lips curved in a grin. "Nicely done, Madam Lares."

His grin warmed away the icy cold that was the aftermath of my battle with the demon.

I frowned. "It nearly killed us all. I don't know what we're going to do if we get swamped with several of those things."

"We'll handle it," Mavis said, taking my hand. "You have a powerful council, honey. We'll all do our part."

"What happened with the voodoo queen?" Ferral asked. "How'd you free her from the vortex?"

"It was Princess Layla." I shrugged. "Or, really, her guards." I told them about the strange rescue operation.

Gren nodded. "Clever. The vortex would have been designed to repel lost ones. By wrapping a lost one around your friend, they ensured it would repel her too."

I nodded. "Layla didn't explain it to me, but that makes sense. She did say that taking Shadee out of there shortened our timetable considerably, though."

Ferral nodded. "That is my concern. We'll need to move fast. We won't get any warning before this thing moves to the next level."

"Let's get back to the church and marshal our forces," I said. "I need to recharge and feed my dog."

Mavis slipped her arm through mine as we headed out the door. "He probably thinks he's dying. It's been hours since he last ate."

We laughed at that. It felt good to think of something normal. I was especially happy that I'd left the little guy safely at home.

Ferral held the door to the back seat of my car open for me and stuck his hand under my nose. "Keys."

I gave him a look.

"You're in no shape to drive, Madam Lares," he said, his tone uncompromising.

I thought about arguing but decided it wasn't worth the effort. He was right. I was beat, and still a little wobbly on my legs. I handed him my keys and slid into the back.

"Shotgun," Mavis called, earning herself a confused look from Ferral.

"Where?" the advocate asked, making us all laugh. That confused him even more.

"She means she wishes to take the front seat," Gren told Ferral with a sparkle in his eye.

Ferral's embarrassed flush was almost better than chocolate. "The human language is ridiculous," he muttered crankily.

Gren slid into the back seat with me. As Ferral started toward home, the protector's warm, strong fingers clasped mine. I was so happy to feel his touch that I nearly forgot to razz my least favorite advocate about something of vital importance. "By the way, Ferral...tookus?"

Mavis barked a peal of delighted laughter.

Ferral flushed again. "The historian has a unique vocabulary. Listening to her drone on and on, I sometimes accidentally learn interesting new words."

"Um-hum," I said, grinning widely. Wanda droning on and on about anything was as likely as Ferral gaining a sense of humor. That was never happening. But it didn't matter. I was perfectly happy to enjoy a laugh or three at his expense.

17

A DEADLY SOUP OF HORRENDOUS THINGS

We stopped by to speak to Chief Marshal on the way home. He was sitting behind his desk, his expression bleak and his shoulders drooping with weariness. He looked up when Gren and I came through the door, frowning. "You look about like I feel," he told me with a grim smile.

I ran a hand self-consciously through my hair, finding it tangled and dusted with tiny shards of glass. "Busy day. How are things going with the prisoners?"

The curve of his lips took a decidedly downward shift. He sighed, running a hand through his salt and pepper hair. "Not good. They're going downhill fast." His gaze caught mine. "Isn't there something we can do to get those things out of them?"

Gren and I shared a glance. The chief didn't miss it. "Who are you?" he asked my protector. "Can you do something to help?"

"He's a friend," I told Chief Marshal. "A member of my council."

"Madam Lares will defeat this evil," Gren said. "You can depend upon her."

"I'm working on it," I told the cop. My voice wasn't too convincing, even to my own ears. "Are the lost ones doing what they're supposed to do?"

He nodded. "They don't say much, do they?"

I really didn't know what one of them was like in a normal...or at least what passed as normal at the moment... setting. I'd only met them on the field of battle, except for Layla. Remembering her brought my spirits low. She'd saved my life when that thing in the senior home attacked. And she might die because of it. "They aren't real chatty, no," I finally said. "But I think we can trust them."

"You think?" His eyes went round with alarm. "Aggy, I've got four creatures in my jail, any one of which could kill me without busting a sweat. I need you to be a little more certain than that."

Biting back a sigh, I said, "Chief, I'm not certain about anything right now. I'm sorry, but that's the truth. I can tell you that their princess just saved my life, and she's currently fighting for hers after battling a demon."

Our gazes tangled for a long moment before he looked away, resting his head wearily in his hands. "What a mess. I wish you'd just left me stupid about all this."

"Then you would have died," I said, my tone relentlessly stark.

His head jerked up at the brutality of my response. Then, amazingly, he nodded. "I'm sorry, Aggy. It's really hard to see those two young people being ravaged like that. I've known them and their parents for years."

"I understand, Chief. I promise you, I'm doing everything I can." I wished I could believe my own words. If I was telling the truth, why did I feel so helpless? Why did I feel like an imposter? I really had no idea what to do about that putrid hole in the ground or the nasty creatures it kept belching into my town. "Has there been any sign of more possessed people?"

"No. I just got back from walking the streets. It seems quiet. Too quiet, if you ask me."

I nodded. I knew just how he felt. The drive over from the senior home had been eerily quiet. Nobody walked the sidewalks in town. Stores were empty. The streets had no cars. The people of Rome might not all be magical, but I couldn't help thinking they'd gained an innate understanding of when to keep a low profile from living side-by-side with magical neighbors. "It feels like the quiet before the storm."

"Exactly," Chief Marshal agreed. "Aggy, I want to help. What can I do?"

"I'm not sure, Chief. I'll let you know, okay?"

His disappointment was clear on his face. "Look, I know I'm just an old cop. I don't know anything about the world you live in. I have nothing to fight with except bullets and fists. But I love this town. My family has lived in Rome for nearly a hundred years. I can't just stand by and watch this... evil...take it down."

I thought about that for a few beats and then nodded. "There may be something you can help with," I told him. "If we're going to defeat this thing, We're going to need everyone's help...magical and non-magical alike."

He straightened in his chair, his broad shoulders squaring. "What do you want me to do?"

"First..." I said, sending a silent call to one of my council. A moment later, Reverend Dodson showed up. The chief flinched, reaching toward a side drawer in his desk. I assumed it was where he kept his gun. His hand stalled, and he shook his head. "I'm not sure I'll ever get used to ghosts popping into my jail."

"Just think of me as your spectrally-inclined friend," Reverend Dodson said with a grin.

"...I want you to work with the reverend to create a sacred circle around Golden Years," I told the chief. "If these things break free, I want them contained until we can kill them. If you can talk the townspeople into helping with a prayer chain, that would be good. But don't try to tell the non-magical about the vortex or the demons. They won't believe you."

Davis sighed.

"The magical will know by now that the town is in danger. They'll let you know who they are."

He jerked his head in understanding.

Glancing at the reverend, I said, "We can use as many religious leaders as you can gather, dead or alive."

He nodded.

"I need you to create consecrated ground around the senior home and supercharge it. Can you do that?"

He inclined his head. "We'll get started right away, Madam Lares."

I nodded at Gren. "We'll get going then. Let me know when it's done." Gren held the door for me and I stopped on the threshold, looking back at the chief. "If you are a man who prays," I told him, "this is a really good time to do it."

I left without waiting for a response, my heart heavy.

Gren and I didn't speak the rest of the way home. My emotions were too close to the surface for words, and he was likely trying to respect my mood. Pulling into the small parking lot at home, I slid out of the car. Slamming the door, I turned to find myself mere inches away from a broad, hard chest. I sucked in a surprised gasp.

Gren looked down at me, his eyes the color of dark chocolate. "You will defeat this scourge, Aggy," he said, his voice husky with emotion. "I have faith in you."

I shook my head, tears burning my eyes. Opening my mouth to deny that I was as strong as he believed I was, I found myself suddenly tugged up against his long, sculpted form.

I pulled a heated, Gren-flavored breath into my lungs and stood stiffly as his arms came around me, wrapping me in a cocoon of warmth and comfort.

After a moment of his not saying anything, I relaxed, letting my body conform to his. He held me like that for a long time. With each passing moment, I felt more like myself, my confidence returning in bits and pieces.

But a new kind of tension zinged along my nerve endings. One that was decidedly more pleasant.

Gren wrapped a warm hand around the back of my neck and an arm around my waist. His heartbeat, slow and steady, sang an addictive song of understanding and acceptance into my ear.

I closed my eyes and sighed. "Thank you. I needed this."

He lowered his head and kissed my temple, the touch of his lips gentle and lingering. "You're welcome, beautiful Aggy."

I finally forced myself to pull away. "We should go in now. The council is here."

Part of my growing Lares magic allowed me to know where my council members were and enabled me to call them to me as needed. The thought made me frown as I remembered I hadn't been able to feel Gren after Ferral had taken him to a healer. That had scared me more than anything.

I headed toward the front door. Gren fell in beside me, his fingers tangling with mine.

Before we went inside, I stopped, turning to him. "Where did Ferral take you to be healed?"

Gren's expression turned rigidly neutral, a warning that he wasn't going to tell me the truth. "To a healer."

"Yes, but where? What healer? I lost track of you."

He reached past me and opened the door, giving it a push. "Do you know any healers, Aggy?"

"No. But I..."

He smiled, and my entire body melted into a puddle at his feet. "Then there is no point in my telling you which healer, is there?"

I narrowed my gaze on him. "That was a Ferral-like response, which means I didn't like it. At all."

"You called?" said a deep, snotty voice from inside the house.

I held Gren's gaze for another beat, willing him to answer my question, and then frowned and turned away. "Thanks for nothing," I muttered to him as I went inside.

Bev hurried over to me when I came inside. "We have a visitor."

My brows lifted. "Who is it?"

"One of the people from Golden Years," she told me. "A Mrs. Wolde. She doesn't talk much. The only way I identified her was by looking through her purse."

"Mrs. Wolde?" I'd completely forgotten about her. She'd been waiting for me on the couch while Mavis and I checked on Shadee. My eyes went wide. Had the shadowy demon scared her off? Or had it hurt her? Panic flared at the thought. "Where is she? Is she okay?" I pushed past my sister.

"In the kitchen. She seems fine."

Bev followed me down the hall to the kitchen, where I learned why my dog hadn't greeted me at the door as he usually did.

Mrs. Wolde was sitting on the floor near the refrigerator, feeding Monty bits of the sandwich she was supposed to be eating. Monty took the nibbles like a gentleman, easing them gently from her fingertips. In between every bite, he shifted on the floor, somehow always ending up a wee bit closer to the plate on her lap.

"Monty," I scolded before scooping him up. I kissed him on the nose and earned myself a lick on the cheek. "Leave it."

He wagged his tail, his bright brown gaze brimming with innocence. I grinned. "Not buying it, little man." I settled him back to his feet and crouched down beside my elderly visitor. "How are you feeling, Mrs. Wolde?"

She gave me a toothless smile. Somewhere along the way, she'd lost her dentures. "I'm fine. Thanks for asking, dear." She patted my knee and took a tiny bite of what looked like a turkey sandwich. She'd pulled the tomato and lettuce out of it and was eating just cheese and turkey inside white bread. I looked up as Bev handed me a plate too. "She fed all the bacon to Monty. He's probably going to be sick later."

I shook my head. "Doubtful. That boy's got a cast-iron stomach." But he did look like he was getting a little wider in the booty than he'd been. Too much people food lately. I'd have to cut him back. Though it was hard to do with everybody around spoiling him all the time.

"Mrs. Wolde, why did you leave Golden Years? Did something scare you?"

She shook her head. "Why would I be scared, dear?"

"I don't know. It's just that you said you were going to

wait for me in the lobby at Golden Years. But you didn't wait."

"I went for a walk."

"A walk?" When she nodded, I asked, "You walked all the way here?"

She took a tiny bite of her sandwich and chewed it for much longer than the bite required. Finally, she swallowed. "I did. I enjoy walking. It's such a pretty day."

I sent a worried frown toward Bev. The distance between the senior home and my house had to be nearly eight miles. I wondered if someone had given her a lift and she'd forgotten. "That's a really long walk." I smiled, trying not to seem like I was scolding. "Your feet must hurt."

The woman fixed rheumy blue eyes on me, a faint smile on her lips. She didn't respond to my comment.

I asked her a few more questions, but she simply nibbled on her sandwich, staring straight ahead with an enigmatic smile on her face.

I stood up and tried to help her to her feet, but she resisted, yanking her arm away several times before I gave up. Short of having one of the men muscle her into a chair, we weren't moving her.

"She doesn't want to sit in a chair," Niele said, his expression grim. "We tried several times."

I nodded. "She has a touch of dementia," I whispered to them.

"I think it might be more than a touch," Bev said, widening her eyes. "I can't believe she found her way here on foot. She's lucky she made it, and we found her."

Eyeing her too slender form, I noted that her feet were bare and filthy. "She was barefoot?"

Bev grimaced, nodding.

Mrs. Wolde had one of my fleece throws around her

shoulders, but the cotton dress she wore was nearly as filthy as her feet. I didn't remember her being that dirty when I saw her at Golden Years, but she had been sitting, and I hadn't paid very close attention to her clothes. "Maybe she sensed the vortex, and her instincts told her to get away from it?"

"That seems plausible," Mavis suggested. "She was in the lobby with that demon thing. She's lucky it didn't kill her."

"Or possess her," Bev added.

We all looked at the woman, watching her entice Monty back over for more bites of her sandwich. She was so gentle with him. Her sweet smile told me she'd had dogs before and enjoyed them. I didn't have the heart to take him away from her. He'd just have to start his diet another day.

Placing my plate on the table, I dropped into a chair with a weary groan.

"You need to eat, honey," Mavis said, handing me a cup of coffee. "You need your strength."

I shook my head and pushed the plate away, gratefully sipping my coffee. "I'm not hungry. But the coffee tastes wonderful. Thanks."

Mavis sent me a look, which I ignored. She'd always been pushy about food. I was usually easy to push since I loved to eat and was always hungry. But, I'd had a day, and I needed to just sit there and infuse my system with caffeine for the moment. "What's going on underground," I asked Niele.

He adjusted his mossy undies and lowered himself into a chair. "It's not good, I'm afraid. There have been some massive ground shifts in town. A few houses on the northern edge are starting to sink."

My eyes flared wide. "Sink? Oh no."

He nodded. "The plates are shifting to take some of the pressure off, but if that thing keeps growing at the speed it currently is, the whole town of Rome might sink beneath the ground before this is over."

My coffee suddenly didn't taste so good anymore. I lowered my head into my hands and closed my eyes. We had to come up with a way to stop the vortex. There was too much at stake if we didn't. I had a thought and my eyes popped open. "Niele, how many of you are there in the area?"

He frowned. "You mean gnomes?"

"Yes."

"Only about ten. But I have family in nearby towns. Some of the others do too. We could probably pull together a few dozen gnomes at short notice. What are you thinking?"

"When you mentioned taking pressure off the plates, it gave me an idea. Do you think the gnomes could create..." I flapped my hands around, trying to come up with the right term. "Natural pressure valves in the earth somehow?"

He thought about that. "It's possible. I can ask our plate specialists."

"Please do that." I grabbed his wrist before he could leave. "Something happened in the woods this morning. I think it might be tied to this shifting you're talking about." I filled them all in on my adventure with the fissure. "It was really terrifying," I told them. "We need to make sure it doesn't happen again. When you bring in your specialists, have them examine that too, please."

He nodded and hurried out the door.

Feeling better for taking steps to remedy at least one issue, I looked at Bev. "Reverend Dodson is going to create consecrated ground around the senior home. Chief Marshal is going to recruit townspeople to pray around the building. Shadee is being cared for, and the jail is still secure."

"What about the lost ones?" Ferral asked. "Do you want me to have them gather around the vortex?"

"I'm not sure yet. Layla left a couple of her people at the senior home to report to her if anything changes. But she's incapacitated now, so..." I stared at my coffee. "I just don't know."

"As I told you before," Ferral said. "Her kind heals much faster than some species. The royals are especially quick healers."

"But will she heal soon enough to be of help?" Bev asked.

Ferral shrugged. "That, I don't know."

My stomach growled, and Mavis glared at me. Sighing, I pulled my plate close. As soon as I took a bite, my body's need to eat took precedence over my mental stress, and I made short work of the sandwich.

Gren stood behind my chair, his comforting warmth radiating across the narrow distance between his skin and mine. My world felt just a little bit better with him there. I was grateful he was back.

The front door opened and slammed closed. Quick footsteps stomped toward us.

I swallowed the last bite of my sandwich and turned as Wanda, Trish, and Luke came in. My eyes went wide when I saw their expressions. "What?"

They shared a look. Wanda slid a glance toward Mrs. Wolde and frowned. "It's okay," I told the teen. "You can talk in front of her."

"A breach has opened up along Main Street," Trish said.

I stood. "What kind of breach?"

"Like a wide ravine filled with fast-moving water," Luke said. "Only…"

"Only what?" I asked.

Wanda fidgeted, her eyes wider than normal. She looked well and truly spooked.

I reached out and took her hands in mine. "Tell me."

"The ravine isn't filled with water." Her voice broke, and she cleared it.

"What is it filled with?" Ferral asked, his tone impatient.

"Blood," Luke said. "It's filled with blood."

18

A GUARDIAN'S LIGHT MUST BURN AND BLAZE

A low, keening sound rose up from the corner where Mrs. Wolde sat. Only, she was no longer sitting. She'd climbed to her feet and was crouching against the wall, her eyes wild and continually skimming the room. The woman's lips moved, but any words she might have spoken were lost beneath the haunting sound of fear.

"What' wr...?" I managed to say, before the first signs of trouble burst over us. Literally. Every light in the house blinked, flared brighter, and then snapped out with a hundred small explosions of sound.

The tension in the room ratcheted into the stratosphere in the blink of an eye.

Monty started to bark, the frantic sound interspersed with the snapping of tiny jaws and a feral growl that sounded like it should be coming from a much larger dog.

In a burst of magical illumination, Ferral exploded into his moon hound form, silver eyes glowing and a companion growl boiling in his broad chest. Monty backed toward the larger dog, his tail whipping frantically, high and tight. It was his aggressive wag.

Another burst of light introduced a massive black wolf with yellow eyes into my kitchen as Luke shifted.

Wanda turned on her heel and ran down the hall, disappearing into my bedroom.

Bev and Mavis chanted softly, their fingers crafting a dual spell on the air in front of them.

Trish popped into her warrior fae form in the blink of an eye.

Gren moved in close to me, pushing me behind him as a hot, putrid wind blew down the hall and hit us hard, nearly shoving me backward into the table.

Pictures crashed off the walls. The clean dishes on the counter were blown to the floor, smashing into pieces and then rising into the air in a tiny whirlwind and flying around the room.

I braced myself and worked at dragging my magic forward as fear pinged along my nerves, making it hard to concentrate.

A long, moaning roar rattled the glass in the windows. The lights flickered again and blew out with a violent burst of sparks.

If the fixtures hadn't been killed before, they had to be well and truly dead after that.

"What's going on?" Trish screamed above the clamor. Her tiny form hovered close to my ear.

"I wish I knew."

The sound of shattering glass slashed my response off at the knees. I knew immediately what that sound meant. "No, no, no, no!" I took off running along the darkened hallway, foul wind pummeling me with every step.

Grabbing the door frame, I swung into the sanctuary

and skidded to a horrified stop, my heart breaking at the sight before me.

My beautiful windows.

All of them.

Shattered.

Glass sparkled in the late afternoon sun, glinting like a billion diamonds scattered over every surface in the large room.

Ferral thundered up the hall and loped into the sanctuary before I could stop him. He jerked to a stop, looking down at the glass sparkling in a beam of sunlight. When he moved again, bright red beads of blood stained the floor where he'd been.

Luckily, his big gray body blocked the door, so no one else could come inside and hurt themselves.

Trish shot into the room above Ferral's head, her tiny staff stretched in front of her, ready to do battle. She jolted to a stop, her tiny wings pounding the air as she gaped around the room. "Goddess bless," she murmured. "Your beautiful windows."

Shadows from the trees outside the broken windows danced along the wall and skated over the detritus of the destruction like manic scarecrows. The heated wind seemed to blow the glooms around the room. Bringing them to horrific life.

One small shadow, separate from the rest, stepped away from the wall and strolled toward me, tail snapping.

Wraith!

I hurried into the room, glass crunching beneath my shoes, and scooped the cat up into my arms. "You idiot feline! You've probably sliced your paws to ribbons."

But there was no blood on Wraith's paws. No visible wounds. The soft pads seemed perfectly fine. I frowned at her and she wriggled for release. "What did you do, cat? Did you float over that glass?"

She worked herself out of my grip and leaped to the floor, unconcerned by the glass as she strode with liquid grace toward the broken remains of my once spectacular window alcove at the end of the room. Once there, she sat down and wrapped her long, coal-black tail neatly around her feet. She sat there staring out at the crossroads beyond my yard, unmoving.

"What is she doing?" Mavis asked from behind Ferral.

"Who knows with that weird creature," Bev responded. She worked her way around the big silver dog, giving his haunches a bump with her hip when he refused to move. "Oh Aggy. This is horrible."

Tears burned my eyes. Repairing all that glass would cost me a fortune. It would probably take every bit of my remaining remodeling budget. And I didn't have a choice. The room was wide open to whatever wanted to come through, including rain and wind and wild creatures.

Something moved in the front yard. I jerked into motion, walking over to look at the tall, muscular form staring out at the crossroads beyond.

Just like Wraith.

Mavis came up beside me. "What's Gren doing?"

I had no idea.

But I was certainly going to find out.

Shoving past Ferral, I wrenched the front door open. "Hey!" I called out as I walked across the lush grass of my front yard. As I always did when enjoying my yard, I gave Niele mental kudos for his excellent greenskeeping work. I needed to remember to tell him that to his face.

If the world would ever stop ending.

Gren turned and watched me approach, his expression

intense.

"What do you see?"

He turned his gaze toward Rome. "You can't see it?"

I shook my head. It looked the same to me. "See what?"

He grabbed me gently by the shoulders and turned me toward the town, his hands a warm weight against my skin. "Use your magic to see," he said, his lips close to my ear. "You are Lares. You have intimate knowledge of the shapes and textures of your dominion. You feel the vibrations of it like a heartbeat. You know the full range of its scents, from the sweet smell of its gardens to the sour stench of fear. By accepting this dominion, you have embraced the nuances of Rome in all its forms."

I stared into a perfect blue sky, dusted lightly with stringy white clouds and a fat, yellow sun that was lowering itself behind the distant horizon as day stumbled toward night. I saw the quaint, well-kept farmhouses on either side of the white gravel band of road stretching between me and my town. I noted the vibrant green fields of soy plants waving in a soft breeze and the tall stalks of corn just starting to turn brown as late summer reached toward fall.

As my magic eased into my vision, the blue sky darkened to muddy gray, the clouds thickening to a threatening black ceiling that hung much lower over the town than it should. Rome was no longer a cheerful silhouette in the near distance.

A putrid yellow fog seemed to envelop it, the fingers of its poisonous effects streaming outward along the roads that led away from town.

Seen with my new sight, the quaint farmhouses tilted at odd angles as if sinking slowly into the earth. The crops drooped their heads...large yellow and brown splotches staining their once healthy leaves.

I forgot to breathe as my gaze followed a particularly dense finger of poisonous magic which led directly to my little piece of heaven. Slowly, dreading what I would find, I turned to look at my home, and felt the world tumble out from under me. "Goddess, no," I murmured, tears burning my eyes.

One side of the structure had sunk several inches into the dirt. The belfry tilted against the ominous gray sky. And the bright white paint was stained yellow...from the poison trying to drag it below the surface.

"That's why the windows broke? Why the electricity short-circuited?"

Gren's warm fingers on my shoulders tightened briefly in response.

Hot tears slipped down my cheeks. I brushed angrily at them. "I'm done with this stupid vortex," I said, my anger giving me strength. I pulled out of Gren's grip and strode toward the house. Throwing open the door, I called out to the council, most of whom were in the main living area, cleaning up glass. "Leave the mess. We have bigger problems."

Wanda came into the room. "Where's your staff? It's not in your bedroom."

I blinked and frowned, my mind blanking on it for a beat. Then I remembered, reaching into my pocket and pulling it out. The staff had shortened even further when I'd stuffed it into my jeans pocket. It was the size of a kitchen knife.

Her eyes went wide. "Snack size. Cool."

I nodded. "And it came to me at Golden Years when I needed it." Which was pretty cool too. I wondered what other really neat things the weapon could do. Too bad it hadn't come with instructions.

"What's going on, honey?" Mavis asked. "Has something else happened?"

"Yes, something else has happened," I said, rage throbbing in my voice. "This Hellmouth situation has gone too far. And we're going to take it down."

And yes, I meant that literally. When I was done with that thing and its nasty minions, they were going to be so deep into the center of the earth they wouldn't be able to blast their way out.

We were gathered in the kitchen since there was still too much glass in the sanctuary. Trish and Luke had somehow managed to board up the windows in that room, but she'd had to use some of the materials she'd stockpiled for my new store and bedroom remodel on the other side of the house.

It didn't matter anyway, since those windows had been shattered too, setting me back thousands more dollars and several weeks of labor.

But I couldn't think about that at the moment. I needed to concentrate on our planning session. "I want full reports from everybody," I told them. "And, just so you know, our timeline has been moved up drastically. The vortex is sucking the entire town down as it grows. We're out of time." I looked at Niele, who, unfortunately, had one of my bath towels wrapped around his hips since he'd apparently forgotten his undies. "How is the release valve project going?"

His frizzy silver hair stuck up in fish fins all over his round head. Clumps of dirt dusted the strands and painted his thick features as he frowned. "Not well, I'm afraid,

Madam Lares. We've lost two under the shifting plates, and the ground is mostly sand beneath that building. Excavating has been a challenge."

My heart sank. "I'm so sorry," I told him. "When this is over, we'll make sure the families of those who are lost are taken care of."

He inclined his head. "We've moved the perimeter further out, where the ground is clay instead of sand. But there's more rock there, which makes it both more treacherous and slower to dig through."

I looked at his hands, frowning at the blood painting the beefy flesh and the torn claws at the tips. Digging through rock couldn't be fun. I nodded. "Have you made any progress at all?"

His scowl told me everything I needed to know. Making a sudden decision, I said, "Change of plans. I want you to move away from the senior home and concentrate on the ground around town. Golden Years is gone. We need to focus on saving Rome. Do whatever you can to protect it."

He nodded and hurried out of the room, handing Mavis his towel as he left the kitchen.

I smiled at the look of horror on her face, noting that it didn't stop her from watching his admittedly fine backside flexing its way down the hall as he left.

I cleared my throat, bringing her guilty face back my way. She winked and smiled.

I glanced at Trish, who was nibbling on a cookie from a bakery box someone, probably Mavis, brought to the meeting. "I'm worried about stopping anything that comes out of that vortex. Is there any kind of trap you can create to at least slow the demons down?"

I'd learned during my seating that the warrior fae were very good at setting complex traps against their enemies.

Trish's traps were unique and sometimes surprising, but they seemed to work exceptionally well.

Trish frowned thoughtfully. "Consecrated ground?"

"Reverend Dodson is working on that as we speak. The sanctification will be buoyed by prayer."

Trish nodded. "I have an idea for something. I'll work with Reverend Dodson on it."

"Okay," I agreed, trusting her to come up with something useful. I glanced at Gren. "You fought a demon. Tell me what we need to beat them one on one."

He leaned against the counter, arms crossed over his chest and a thoughtful look on his well-crafted face. Something stirred in my center when I looked at him. Something that made me wish all the crazy would stop for a while so I could spend time exploring his effect on me. Shaking off the thought, I waited for his response, which didn't come for a full minute. "As I'm sure you've figured out, we're dealing with different levels of demons."

I nodded. "The ones who possessed that young couple don't seem to be as strong as the one you battled."

"Or the one at the senior home," Mavis added.

"Right." That reminder made my nerves prickle and my stomach twist with remembered fear. "That one was bad."

Gren nodded. "The lesser demons, such as those who need a host to function on this plane, are relatively easy to defeat. Working together, we should have no trouble taking them down."

"So far, at least, there aren't many of them," Bev said.

Gren shook his head. "We mustn't assume that," he told her. "They are good at hiding in plain sight until it's time to show themselves."

Bev frowned.

I knew how she felt. If the host-requiring demons were

capable of hiding themselves, we could discover that they've infected a whole lot of the population of Rome. "How do we kill the demons without harming the hosts?"

The narrow door leading to the belfry opened, and Wanda stepped into the kitchen, "You can't," she said.

My dog jumped up from his favorite spot beneath the table and ran over to her, his tail wagging in enthusiastic greeting.

The soft fluttering of wings sounded from the narrow stairwell. A beat later, the bat fluttered into the kitchen.

Bev grimaced and shuddered. "Dang flying rodent."

In an apparent response to her blasphemy, the bat flew right at her face and soared over her head as she ducked with a scream.

The bat chirped happily at her response, then circled the room once and settled onto the light fixture above the table. The creature's large, yellow eyes glowed with magic as it stared at me.

"No pooping on my kitchen table," I told it.

The bat chirped again. I was learning the creature liked to get the last word.

"What did you mean," I asked. "...about not killing the demons?"

Wanda opened the fridge and pulled out a soda, popping the top and drinking deeply before answering me. "Bathilda and I have been conferring upstairs..."

"Bathilda?" I asked, grinning. I glanced at the creature hanging upside down from my light. "Nice. Can I call you Batty for short?"

Bev snorted out a laugh and then winced when the bat spun its scary yellow gaze to her.

"That's not her real name. It's just a nickname," Wanda said.

"What's her real name?" I asked, staring at the secretive creature. I knew bats didn't talk, but neither did dogs, yet Ferral managed to give me snotty advice in my mind when he was in his moon hound form. It would be nice if the bat, who gave even Ferral a run for his money in evasiveness, communicated once in a while.

"She won't tell me," Wanda said. "Now, about those demons, the histories say that hosting doesn't involve the demon's life force laying on top of the human's soul. They actually infuse themselves into the human's essence, changing it incrementally with every passing day."

"So it's a parasitic possession?" Luke asked.

I glanced at the wolf shifter, who was sprawled in a small chair he'd brought from the living room after hopefully de-glassing it. He didn't usually talk much during our meetings. He generally just listened until he had something to say and kept his input short and to the point. But even so, he'd been quieter than usual since the vortex formed an open sore in the senior center.

Wanda nodded. "Which means that, if we can't remove the demon fairly soon after it takes possession, the human host is usually so damaged they don't survive the removal."

"But how do we remove the demon?" Luke asked, "Not theoretically, but specifically. I need a concrete plan."

Wanda nodded. "Methods that are mentioned in historical records are holy water and exorcism spells." She stared at Luke. "That's it."

"The local witch covens can do exorcisms, but there will be logistical issues," Bev said.

I frowned. "What do you mean?"

"With the exception of the couple in the jail, we don't even know who's been possessed."

"And," Mavis added, "they won't be in a single place

either. If townspeople are affected, they're going to come from all over Rome. How do we plan for that?"

"A large-scale trap spell," Trish said, her eyes alight with inspiration.

Bev and Mavis perked up with interest. "Do we have the witch-power to do that?" Bev asked.

"I think so," Trish answered, nodding. "The sum, in this case, is much greater than the parts. We can talk about the specifics in more detail in a smaller group of coven members, but what I'm thinking is a basic demonic expulsion hex with an incantation enhancer spell laid over it."

"That might work," Mavis agreed.

"But what's the trigger?" Ferral asked.

"We can use the demon's specific magical signature in our spells. Then, anytime one of them moves into the spell area, the trap springs."

Mavis frowned. "Then what? We can't isolate the demon form once it leaves the host. How are we going to expel it?"

"We could use sanctified ground," Ferral said.

"Good idea," I agreed. "So, I need the Reverend to sanctify the entire town," I said, wondering if he could manage it. I needed to speak to him. I added that to my mental list, fighting a weary sigh. "How can you get each demon's specific signature to make the spell work?" I asked.

Mavis shook her head, smiling. "That's the beauty of this type of demon," she said. "They're like livestock in the demonic plane. They don't even have unique signatures. They were created, not born, so they all share the same magical footprint. It will be like shooting demons in a barrel."

"You ladies can get that set up?" I asked, starting to feel better about the idea.

"Yes," Trish looked at her coven sisters. "Let's call a senior coven member meeting to iron out the details."

"Trish, are we spreading you too thin?" Luke asked. "You were going to work with the rev too."

She shook her head. "I'll just help the witches lay out the spell, and then I can transition to the other stuff."

"Let me know if you get overwhelmed," I told her. "We can't afford to drop any balls with this."

She nodded.

"What's our timeline?" Bev asked, glancing at the clock.

I looked at Ferral and Gren. "We need to move fast, but we have to allow ourselves enough time to finish our preparations."

Ferral crossed his beefy arms over his chest, his legs stretched out beneath the table. "Midnight," he said. "When the magic is highest. That's when they'll make their move."

I looked at the clock. We only had a few hours to prepare and set up. "Is the vortex really that far along?"

Gren nodded. "I'm afraid so. The shadow demon we battled at Golden Years is one of their most powerful. They don't usually arrive until the evolution is nearly complete. We're within hours of this vortex becoming a Hellmouth and taking over Rome."

We thought about that for a long moment, the expressions in the group running the gamut of scared, worried, thoughtful, and angry. But Ferral pretty much always looked angry, so I wasn't sure that counted.

A sudden thought brought me up out of my chair, surging to my feet so I could see past the table to the corner near the fridge.

"What is it?" Gren asked, stepping closer.

I turned my horrified gaze to him. "Where's Mrs. Wolde?"

19

TO FORGE A PATH FOR BRIGHTER DAYS

"We haven't talked about how to close the abyss," Gren said.

I lunged forward, swinging my staff toward a distant tree and then lifting one foot and spinning to focus it on another target. The warm-up exercises helped me center my mind in preparation for using the staff's intimidating magic.

At least, they would have if I didn't have a sexy distraction staring at me. "I'm working on that."

After hours of talking and planning, it felt good to use my muscles for a while. I took a short break, wiping my sleeve over my sweaty brow.

Gren's dark brown gaze held mine, their depths warming. "You're not going to fling yourself into the abyss," he said.

I averted my gaze, lifting my staff to point the orb at a stack of cans Niele had set up for my target practice between the house and the woods. The target was far enough away that I had to bleed a little energy into my eyes to sharpen my sight, but close enough that I felt confident any blow-back would miss damaging anything important.

"Aggy?" his tone held censure when I averted my gaze rather than respond.

"I've got this," I told him, sending a dense stream of golden energy into the can wall and blasting it to smithereens. I grimaced. "I might have put too much into that one."

He didn't chuckle as I'd hoped. "Aggy, I won't let you sacrifice yourself to that vortex."

I turned forty-five degrees to the right and concentrated on the wall of tree branches representing my second target. Concentrating harder than I had the first time, I managed a less dense stream of energy that only demolished half of target two.

Better.

Not perfect.

"Stop ignoring me," Gren said with uncharacteristic crankiness.

"I'm not. I'm practicing with my staff, so I don't have to fling myself into the vortex," I responded angrily.

The truth was that I didn't have a clue how to defeat the vortex. I only knew that I was the one who had to close it. Nobody else could do it.

I knew deep down in my gut that, if it came down to only one option...the option of flinging myself into the abyss...I'd do it. Because the idea of failing the people I'd been called to protect made me want to chew off my own arm. I'd never be able to live with myself if I took the safe route, and the people of Rome paid the price.

But no way was I going to tell Gren that.

I swung my gaze to the last target. The pile of rocks reached five feet in height and was ten feet wide. I could blast it with full power and it would present an impressive spectacle. But I was good at blasting stuff to smithereens. It didn't take an expert to do that. What was hard was using a deft touch. I was really bad at that.

I pointed the staff at the rocks. The orb on the end flared brightly when it caught its target and then settled down to a low simmer as it waited for my direction. I closed my eyes, thinking of the two fawns I'd pulled from the fissure, wrapped in delicate strands of gold energy.

That was the level of finesse I needed to cultivate.

Feeling the energy ease into a slow pulse rather than a rabid rush, I opened my eyes again and eyed the rock sitting at the top of the target. It was probably twenty pounds of quartz rather than limestone. Not as easily blown apart. I pulled air into my lungs and slowly released it, allowing my control over the magic to ease just slightly.

A thin stream of energy slid from the orb, shooting toward the rock.

Too fast!

I gripped the pulse with my mind and it slowed, fighting me every inch of the way. Picturing what I wanted to do, I carefully wrapped the shimmering gold string around the rock.

I lifted the end of the staff just a tiny bit, and the rock lifted too. Sweat slid down my face and dripped onto my shoulder. I lifted it higher and ground it to a stop. My teeth were clenched from the effort. A comforting warmth slipped over my back, and strong hands found my shoulders. "Breathe, Aggy," Gren said in a husky whisper.

The sound of that command was nearly my undoing. The rock plunged downward and jerked to a stop as I wrenched control back at the last possible moment.

I inhaled a long, slow breath, expelled it just as slowly,

and then lifted the rock again. I stopped lifting it when it was three feet above the target.

"Nicely done, Madam Lares," a deep voice said behind me.

I yelped, lost focus, and the rock slammed into the wall hard enough to break several of the stones beneath it. Rock dust puffed into the air and the target rock rolled down the pile, clunking loudly from one stone to the next until it plopped onto the ground.

I turned to glare at Ferral.

He lifted his blond brows. "You need to work on achieving better focus," he said, his tone a sea of arrogance that I wanted to drown him in.

"What do you need?" I asked the advocate through gritted teeth.

"We have visitors," he said, frowning.

I didn't want to know what type of visitor would make Ferral frown. He usually believed he could handle any comers all by himself.

"Who is it?"

He shook his head. "You'll want to see this for yourself." The impossible man turned and strode back toward the house. I eyed the fallen rock, wondering if I could pick it up again with my magic and clock him on the head with it.

"Don't bother," Gren said, reading my intentions. "You'll just pulverize the rock on his hard skull. Then you won't be able to practice with it anymore."

My laughter was ruthlessly cut off when his mouth dropped suddenly to mine. I gasped as the touch of his soft lips turned my system nuclear, melting me in all the right places.

Without hesitation, I turned into him and wrapped my arms around his neck, drawing myself as close as I could get while his devastating mouth did things to me that had never been done before.

I forgot the staff, which had dropped from my nerveless fingers as soon as Gren's mouth lowered to mine. The world slid away behind a gilded cocoon that included only him and me. Not even Ferral's arrogant gamesmanship could invade the magical space.

But, like all exquisite things, the pleasure didn't last nearly long enough.

Gren pulled away from me, his eyes molten pools that held me locked in place as he whispered. "You can stop this evil, Aggy. I know you can. But I promise, if you throw away your life, I will haunt your afterlife for all eternity."

Funny, I thought. That didn't seem like much of a threat. I could definitely think of worse ways to spend my afterlife than being stalked by Gren.

I HATED TO ADMIT IT, but Ferral was right. I needed to see the collection of creatures standing on my front lawn. It would have been a shame to miss it.

I glanced from the two lost ones standing at the base of the steps and then let my gaze slide over the dozen or so of them arrayed in formation across my lawn.

Unlike the last time I'd had their kind in my yard, the current group was clearly from Princess Layla's... court?...rather than being of the meaner variety that had tried to kill us all.

I recognized the two guards from the courtyard at Golden Years and walked down the steps to speak to them. "How is she?" I asked. "The princess?"

The male's wide brow crinkled, the skin around his eyes tightening. "She…is healing."

Worry for the creature who'd come to me for an alliance made my stomach tighten with fear. "Is there something I can do to help?" I took a step closer, but Ferral placed a hand on my arm, stopping me.

"Why are you here," he asked the male.

I threw him a glare, but he ignored me as usual.

The female inclined her head, her black horns more delicate than the male's and a lighter shade. They were more charcoal gray than black. Like Layla's, her skin was dove gray, and her form was less bulky. She was several inches shorter than the male. I put him at something over seven feet tall. "Our princess requires that we assist you in the coming war," the female told us.

"War?" I asked. I thought about it and realized that, though I'd been avoiding thinking about it that way. A war was exactly what we were about to engage in. "I'd be very grateful for your help."

The female nodded as if I'd simply stated the obvious.

"The call has gone out," the male said.

Beside me, Ferral tensed. Gren stepped up on my other side, and the rest of my council filed out of the house to stand behind me.

"The call?" I asked.

Gren was the one who answered my question. "The vortex has reached its full strength. It is calling demonic warriors on both planes to come to the battle."

My knees weakened underneath me. "From here too?"

He nodded, his expression carefully neutral. "The lost ones feel the call, even though we're not demons."

There was no outward reaction in the creatures arrayed before us. Layla had told me her people wanted to stay on the human plane, but I wondered if that was entirely true. There had to be some who'd like to go back to the demonic plane. If so, however, the lost ones in my yard gave no indication of it.

Wings fluttered above my head. I didn't look up as the raven settled onto my shoulder. He opened his black beak and cawed, the sound strangely amplified.

The bird's vocalizations niggled something in my memory, and I had a sudden thought. I glanced at Ferral. "Can we use the key to call the celestial army?" In the final test of my seating, I'd discovered that the raven held the key to open the gates of Nirvana.

Ferral shook his head. "They won't come. This is your dominion. You must defend it yourself."

The response was delivered in a cold tone, the words stark against the silence. It was pure Ferral. But I knew he was right. It would be nice if someone would come and fight the battle for me. If someone would keep my council safe from the fate we had laid out in front of us. But, apparently, that wasn't the way it was done.

I inclined my head. "Understood." I looked at the two spokes-demons...and said, "Come around back, and we'll discuss what you can do to help us." They wouldn't be able to come into the church because it was built on sanctified ground. But my little patio was a good neutral zone.

Without another word, the two emissaries turned on their heels and headed around the house.

20

OR LET THE DARKNESS RISE AND RULE

I stood in the garden Niele had created for me, eyes closed and body surprisingly relaxed. Monty bounced around the nearby tombstones, tail wagging, chasing something I couldn't see. It was probably one of the ghosts, playing a game of tombstone tag with him...a game all parties seemed to enjoy.

The thought made me smile.

The sweet scent of an array of different flowers rose up around me, the cool night air doing nothing to suppress the comforting scents.

Wraith bumped against my calves and moved on toward the graveyard, where I had no doubt she'd do her best to tease my dog.

For just a moment...a comfortable blip in time...my world felt good and solid and filled with the sweet joy of just being alive.

Then I remembered the whispered conversation I'd had with Princess Layla's guards before they left, and reality came crashing down as I realized that I'd set something into motion which would probably get me killed. We were moments away from going to war. A war that had been foisted upon us, and one that I didn't know whether we'd win. My eyes snapped open and I inhaled the sweetly scented air, pulling it into my lungs as a barrier to the stench of evil to come.

My cell phone rang. I answered it without looking at the screen. "Yes?"

"Aggy?"

I frowned. "Is everything okay at the jail?" I asked Chief Marshal.

"The possessed are unconscious in the cell. But, I wanted to let you know that the lost ones have disappeared. Nobody's watching that poor young couple in there."

My eyes closed as the first niggling concerns about the alliance rolled over me. Had I made a terrible mistake? What if Layla was setting us up to fail? Or, maybe even worse, what if her people were taking the opportunity of her being hurt to engage in a revolt?

"Where are you?" I asked Davis.

"In the jail wing. Somebody has to keep an eye on them."

"Did you and Reverend Dodson complete your other mission?"

"We did. Everything's in place."

"Good. Then lock up the jail as best you can and get out of there. If they wake up and try to escape, you won't be able to stop them."

"I can't do that, Aggy. This jail and its prisoners are my responsibility."

"And everyone's safety is mine. I need you to help me keep the townspeople safe tonight, Chief."

"What about these two?" he asked, a growl in his voice. He clearly wasn't happy with me.

I thought about what to say. Telling him there were probably a lot more like them in town wasn't going to make him feel any better, but it might help him understand why I was asking him to abandon his post. Still, I knew Chief Marshal, and I doubted he'd do as I asked unless I gave him a darn good reason to. "The witches are working right now on blanketing the town in a spell to exorcise the demons. We've got the possessed part of this equation covered. But there are bigger, badder problems coming, Chief. It's going to take all of us to deal with those."

Silence met my argument. I waited tensely for his response. I didn't know why it felt important for him to leave the jail. But somehow, it did.

"Okay, Aggy. I'll leave."

"Thanks," I said, meaning it. Hanging up, I slipped my phone into the pocket of the leather jacket I was wearing. Smoothing my sweaty palms down the matching leather pants, I grimaced, feeling like a fraud in the superhero garb. Bev and Mavis had talked me into the clothes a few weeks after my seating. They'd argued, correctly, that the leather garb would keep me safer than regular clothes when I went up against the big baddies. Still, it felt strange to be wearing them. Between the leather, the flat black boots that molded to my calves, and the high, bouncy ponytail I'd chosen so I wouldn't have to battle my hair during whatever happened later, I felt like a totally different Aggy than usual. A fact that wasn't sitting lightly with me given everything else I was worried about.

I caught movement in the darkness shrouding the woods at the back of my property. Used to trouble coming out of the Mystical Wood, my gaze whipped in that direction and energy sparked in my core, spitting into the might from my fingertips.

At first, I saw nothing. I stood staring into the darkness with my heart pounding hard against my ribs. Then, just as a bank of clouds cleared the full moon high above us, two unexpected creatures stepped out of the shadows.

Bathed in the pure wash of the fat silver moon, the twin fawns stood tall and proud, no longer adorable babies, but full-grown deer with fur silvered by magic and, in the case of the male, the largest rack of antlers I'd ever seen. They were spectacular and somehow comforting. They didn't move a muscle, just stood there, half a football field away from me, and stared into my eyes, their own beautiful gazes sparking with golden light.

The door to the house slammed closed behind me. I sucked in a breath, certain they would run. They didn't startle at the sound. They didn't even turn their attention away from me. Though no communication happened between us, I somehow knew why they were there. They wanted me to know that I was strong enough, worthy enough, smart enough.

Even as my usual doubts flooded in, trying to negate the message of support and respect, my muscles lost some of their tension. I pulled air into lungs that suddenly didn't resist filling. And the pulse that had begun to pound when I thought of the coming war soothed in my veins.

Without warning, Ray dropped from the sky and landed lightly on my shoulder. He danced around for a moment, his feathers ruffling and then settling back into place. The bird cast his beady black gaze on the deer and then clacked his beak, finally sending a strident call into the night.

A call to battle.

Warmth bathed my side, and I turned to find Gren standing there. "Ready?"

I nodded. My gaze slid back to the deer and I blinked,

disappointed. They were gone. They'd slipped back into the darkness as if they'd never been there. For a moment, I wondered if they had. Maybe I was grasping for anything to calm my churning soul. Maybe I'd imagined them.

Gren handed me my staff. "Wanda told me I should give this to you."

I nodded, turning with him and heading back to the house. "She's still here?"

"No." He wrapped an arm around my waist and tugged me close. "She left a few minutes ago." He frowned. "She's managing to stay quite a bit longer these days."

"She traveled to Golden Years with me earlier."

He looked surprised. "Maybe the witches are affecting the hex."

"I hope so. It breaks my heart to see her struggling to be part of the council when she has no control over most of her life."

Gren opened the door for me. "Has she told you where she goes when she's not here?"

"She won't tell me anything. I'm starting to realize it was a miracle when I got her to talk about how she came to be hexed."

He stepped aside as Monty barreled past him, running to his empty bowl with futile hope. "Let's get this current issue behind us, and I'll try to find out more."

"I don't want to invade her privacy," I warned, torn between wanting to know she was okay and not wanting to stick my nose where it wasn't welcome.

"Understood. I'll be restrained in my investigations." Gren waited as I got my littlest hero a dog cookie to soften the sting of being left behind.

Then, having stalled as long as I could, I looked around. "Where is everybody?"

"They're already in place."

I nodded, my heart pounding with anticipation and dread. "I guess we should go then." Heading toward the front door, I was pulled to a stop when Gren grabbed my hand. I turned to him, frowning. "What?"

"We're not taking the car."

"Why not?"

He tugged me toward the back door. "So many reasons. Most important is that the roads aren't safe. The townspeople will expect you to come that way. It would be too easy for them to ambush you."

Ice filled my chest at his words. He was speaking like the entire town was already possessed. What if he was right?

My wide eyes must have given away my panic. Gren tugged me through the door, his voice soothing. "We don't know how many have been affected. We're just being cautious. If we meet possessed humans outside of the trap, we'll have fewer options for defeating them without causing lethal harm."

That made sense. "Okay." I felt a grin tugging my lips. "So, it's Air Gren then?"

Standing in the grass just past the patio, he smiled, the sight melting the ice in my chest and flash-heating my blood in the blink of an eye. With the sound of a mainsail catching the wind and snapping taut, Gren's enormous wings exploded into existence and lifted above his head before settling. "Climb aboard, Madam Lares."

I walked over and wrapped myself around his back, my arms around his shoulders, and my legs around his waist. I already knew I would be flying first class. "What's the movie tonight?" I asked.

"Breathless," he said before taking three leaping strides

and shooting into the air, leaving the sound of my squealing behind in lieu of a vapor trail.

Gren set us down in a small copse of trees near Golden Years. I was shaken by the flight, not because I'd ridden on the back of a man with giant wings, that part had been fun, but because, even in the darkness, I'd been able to see the blood-filled gash in the earth that Trish, Luke, and Wanda had told us about. The horror-inducing river flowed down the middle of Main Street and kept going, running as far as I could see out into the country.

Not good.

I realized I was looking at another one of the reasons I hadn't been able to drive into town. I could understand why Gren hadn't led with that. It was a chilling sight.

I discovered something even more startling than that bloody fissure when we landed.

Golden Years was...gone.

The entire building had sunk beneath the surface of the earth, leaving behind a Hellmouth that no longer lay upon the ground like a giant, stinking puddle.

It had become something much more terrifying. A building-sized, roughly rectangular hole in the world's fabric. The festering boil on the surface of the world rose thirty feet into the air, its bubbling surface cutting the stars from the sky like a giant cookie cutter.

The center roiled and spit, occasionally belching out another horrible, misshapen abomination that mostly disintegrated into a pile of ash when it hit the sanctified ground Reverend Dodson had created.

Still, looking at the shimmering surface of the Hellmouth and feeling the malevolence of the thing, it was a wonder that Chief Marshal and the handful of townspeople still stood beyond its grip, bibles in hand and mouths moving in prayers I couldn't hear.

I doubted even they could hear their own prayers. The vortex gave off a constant drone, like the sound of a thousand victims moaning in pain, and punctuated by an irregular chorus of terror-filled screams.

The entire package was unspeakably alarming.

Ray fluttered down to my shoulder and clacked his beak in greeting. I reached up and touched his sleek feathers, my gaze never leaving the sight before me. Swallowing hard, I clutched the staff in my hand so hard my palm ached. I concentrated on loosening my grip.

Heat coated my back as Gren moved in behind me. He didn't touch me, and I was glad. At that moment, the smallest offering of comfort would be my undoing. I longed for an excuse to be swaddled in protection. Even while knowing I couldn't give in to that need.

"Are you ready, Madam Lares?"

I closed my eyes, my chest painfully tight as the breath caught in my lungs and refused to move. I pushed past the barrier of fear with monumental effort, burying it deep to fill my chest with air. "Yes." My voice sounded breathy and broken.

We started forward. To distract myself, I checked in with my team.

Ferral?

Madam. We are standing guard at the Hellmouth. Anything that survives the blessed zone will face the wolf and me.

You'll protect the chief and the people praying?

Of course.

It was one of those rare times when his arrogance reassured rather than annoyed me.

Thank you, advocate. I thought I felt him smile.

Niele?

Madam Lares. We are in place. The release valve operation was a success. The city is no longer sinking. The gnomes lie in wait to catch anything that makes it out of the consecrated field and heads toward Rome.

Trish?

Both traps are set. We're waiting.

Mavis? Bev?

We have a dozen witches, Bev reported. Rome is secured, but nothing is stirring.

Their reports were reassuring. But there was still one facet of our plan that hadn't been engaged. I looked at Gren. "The lost ones?"

He frowned. "They have not been heard from since our earlier meeting."

"Do you think the princess called them off?"

"If she did, she's a fool," he growled out. His tone told me he wouldn't take the slight in stride. He'd do something about it. Despite her saving my life at the senior home, I was pretty sure I'd be right there with him.

The princess knew how much we needed their help.

I shook off my doubts and shoved them away as the vortex suddenly bulged outward in the center, its shiny surface stretching to the point that I could see something with a beak and skeletal form raking its way free of the energy surrounding it.

Then, with a shriek that turned my blood to ice, the demon burst from its surface and took to the air.

Curse, swear, curse, curse, curse! A flying demon. Goddess help us. We hadn't prepared for that.

21

RELENTING MEANS SHE PLAYS THE FOOL

Gren sprouted wings and shot into the sky before I had time to stop him. Fear ate a path through my belly, the memory of how he'd come out of the last sky-bound battle with a powerful demon all too fresh in my mind.

Ray took off too, cawing into the night as he winged his way toward the flying demon. I frowned after the raven, wondering what he thought he could do against something as big as that beaked monstrosity.

Then, I didn't have time to worry about Gren because the abyss bulged outward again, another evil boil festering in its gut. As the elasticity of the surface finally broke, a gorgeous white horse flew free of it, landing gracefully in the center of the consecrated field.

The horse stood there snorting and pawing the ground, its sleek sides heaving.

I started forward, my gaze locked on the creature sitting astride the horse's back.

As if I'd called its name aloud, the demon turned to me and smiled, its bright green gaze glowing in the night. The demon was too beautiful to be real. He wore a pristine suit of white. His white-blond hair, hanging to his waist in sleek waves, danced around his square jaw as he tugged on the reins and sent the ghostly horse into a gallop with a kick of his clean white boots.

Its nostrils flaring with excitement, the horse's matching green gaze burned through the darkness as it thundered in my direction. The beautiful creature's coat was a white so pure it glowed in the dark. Its mane fell almost to its knees, and its tail was a dense, white curtain billowing behind as it ran.

I jolted to a stop and lifted my staff, body braced on my toes so I could leap away if the horse threatened to trample me.

I stared into the eyes of the oncoming creature and willed it to veer. The horse's broad chest bunched with massive muscles and it lowered its head, kicking up grass as it rampaged in my direction.

I had no doubt the beautiful creature was as much the victim of its rider as any of the demon-possessed in Rome. "I don't want to kill you," I whispered, my heart aching at the thought. But I might not have a choice.

Yanking magic from my core, I eased it through the staff until the orb glowed in soft response. If I kept my strike zone narrow, maybe the horse would be spared.

The white demon floated above his mount, sitting lightly astride its back as if he'd lived his entire life on the back of a horse. His smile was wide, teeth white in the soft glow of magic singing through the air.

I fired a stream of sizzling golden energy where his head should have been. But he ducked sideways, easily regaining his balance as horse and rider thundered onward.

I prepared to fire again, my confidence bent, but, as they

came within ten feet of me, the white horse suddenly veered away, just enough to miss me.

But they didn't miss me.

Thigh muscles bulging with effort beneath the white suit, and with one hand wrapped in the horse's mane, the demon leaned down as they passed, snatching me off the ground and dragging me effortlessly onto the horse.

With a yelp of frustration and fear, I dropped my staff.

The white demon's smug laughter coated my spine in ice. The creature holding me against him might look like Prince Charming, but I knew better. He'd been hatched in the deepest bowels of Hell, his soul as black as his heart.

I smacked him hard in the nose with the heel of my hand, infusing my strike with energy, and his head snapped back. He grunted in pain, and his pretty smile turned upside down.

Reaching past him as we galloped wildly through the dark, I called my staff back to me with one hand and yanked on the reins with the other.

The horse screamed with fear, rearing up and flinging us off its back. I slammed into the hard ground, all the breath knocked out of my lungs.

The sound of retreating hooves made me smile as I reached for my magic. The demon had lost his ride.

With a manic cackle, the white demon yanked me off the ground and onto my feet. I gagged and wheezed, still trying to breathe.

"Madam Lares, I presume," said the demon with a disturbingly smooth, deep voice. "It's my pleasure to make your acquaintance." He offered me a mocking bow, and I kicked his knee. Since I'd put a little magic into that kick, there was a very satisfying crack as the bones shifted. He howled, punching me in the face.

I hit the ground again. The demon was immediately on me, his too-handsome face contorted with rage. "That was a mistake, Madam Lares," he growled out. "Now we get to play together, you and I."

"That doesn't sound like fun," I said, one hand over my nose in an attempt to staunch the bleeding.

"I assure you, it won't be." The demon wrapped a large hand around my throat and squeezed, cutting off my air. I forgot about using my magic and clawed at his hand.

Stars burst before my eyes, turning to dancing black dots as I fought to breathe through my constricted throat. I tore at his hand, ripping bloody tracks in his skin. He didn't seem to notice. My flailing legs connected with his stick and berries and, for a quick second, he loosened his grip. I threw out a hand and called for my staff. The shorter version of my weapon slammed into my palm and I stabbed the orb into him at the base of his throat.

Screaming with the effort, I blasted a thick wave of power into the creature's throat.

His eyes bulged. His face turned purple. His perfect lips formed into a surprised "oh" and he convulsed violently over me.

A voice called my name, the sound barely piercing the fog of rage around me. The thing on top of me twisted, contorting, and shriveled into something that no longer looked like a man.

On some level, I knew I should stop pelting him with energy, but the thought-numbing fear of the last couple of days had grabbed hold of me and I couldn't seem to reel myself in.

A warm hand touched my shoulder. "Aggy, you need to stop. You're hurting yourself."

Gren's deep, kind voice finally got through to me. I dug

in, clenching my teeth against the effort to obstruct the magic at my core, and the flow of energy finally snapped off. My hand fell away from the twisted mess lying across my body.

I fell back, panting.

The weight of the dead demon lifted away, and I heard it hit the ground in the distance.

Gren pulled me into his arms and kissed my forehead. "Are you all right?"

I gulped air, clenching my shaking hands. "Yeah. I'm good. Don't I look good?"

Gren snorted out a laugh. "Honestly, you look a bit frazzled."

"You should see the other guy," I said.

I gave him a smile that would probably scare small children. "I might have overreacted a bit. I'm much calmer now."

He winced. "Good. Because we need to close this vortex. It's spewing out nasties faster than we can kill them."

I bit back a groan. "Okay. I'm just going to take a little nap first. Maybe have a PB&C sandwich."

Gren helped me stand. "I promise I'll make you two peanut butter and potato chip sandwiches after this. The nap, though, will have to wait just a little bit."

"Slave driver."

He pulled me into a hug. "I don't want you to do this next part either. But no one else can close the vortex."

I let myself enjoy the embrace for a minute and then gently disengaged from it. "Let's go."

We turned to look as the sound of hooves approached. The gorgeous white horse galloped in our direction and slowed, trotting closer.

Gren suddenly had a long blade in his grip. I covered his hand with mine. "No."

The horse stopped a few feet away and nickered softly, lowering its head.

"It's okay, beauty. I understand." I held out my hands and the horse slowly approached. I rested my forehead against its silky head. "Would you mind giving us a lift?"

The horse nickered. I took that as agreement.

"I'll give you a hand up," Gren offered.

"Wait, just a second." I frowned. "Have the other demons been coming out of that thing on horses, or flying?"

"Those that came out of the Hellmouth mostly have. We've had a rush of earth-bound lost ones to deal with too. They're coming on foot but they're avoiding consecrated ground. Why?"

In the distance, the roaring and screaming had become so pervasive it was almost white noise.

"The demons knew we were going to create that consecrated field." I turned to him. "How did they know that?"

Understanding lit his gaze, he looked suddenly uncomfortable.

"What is it? What aren't you telling me?"

"The witches' trap in town failed. The demons left before it was set."

I stroked a hand over the horse's snowy flank. The action soothed my nerves, allowing me to think more clearly. "They knew. Someone had to have told them."

"You're thinking Layla?" Gren asked.

"I don't know who else could have done it. The council wouldn't have told them."

"One of the witches?" Gren offered.

I shrugged. "We'll need to talk to Bev and Mavis. If

there's somebody in the covens who bends toward dark magic, they should know."

"Caw!" I looked up as Ray fluttered overhead, the sound of his call strident with fear.

I was out of time. "We need to go," I told Gren. My heart was heavy as he boosted me into the saddle and leaped up behind me. I knew what I needed to accomplish. I knew how I wanted to accomplish it. But I didn't have the one thing I needed to get it done.

Clutching the staff in my hand, I spurred the horse into a run, praying that final thing would arrive in time. And that it would be enough.

That *I* would be enough.

We flew across the grass toward the vortex. The white horse's strides were so smooth we barely moved in the saddle. The creature was moving so fast, I wouldn't have been surprised if wings had sprouted from its back.

We skidded to a halt not too far from the consecrated field, when a demon rose up from behind a bush and hissed at us. The thing's slimy black form was squat and squishy, with too many arms and legs that were bent like cabinet handles. Its feet were more claw than flesh.

Gren leaped gracefully off the horse and slashed toward the creature with his blade, easily dispatching it in a spray of goo that plastered his pretty dark hair to his face, dripping off his chin.

The goo smelled like skunk.

"Ew!" I said, grimacing. "That's nasty."

The bushes around us rustled, and several more squishy demons popped out. Ray dove from the sky and attacked one of the nasty creatures, as Gren tucked into two more and the white horse started kicking them like soccer balls.

I jumped down from the horse just as a fresh spate of

screaming started. Something that looked like an upright praying mantis had hold of a woman and was trying to take a bite out of her with its unhinged jaws. Even from where I stood, I could see the thing's nasty set of teeth that looked too big for its tiny head.

I started in that direction, my staff glowing on a fresh wave of energy, just as Ferral leaped on the buggy demon and ripped its nasty head off.

Crisis averted.

For the moment.

We're getting the townspeople out of here, Ferral growled in my head. *It's too dangerous.*

I agree, I responded.

"Get to the vortex!" Gren screamed in between slashes of his blade.

The horse drop-kicked another demon, sending it spiraling to a fiery death near the face of the vortex.

I knew I couldn't stall any longer. Layla apparently wasn't coming.

My heart sank at what that meant...for me...for my family...for my council.

A single tear slid down my cheek as I skimmed Gren a last glance, saying goodbye in a whisper he had no hope of hearing.

Then I turned away and started to run toward the Hellmouth, my heart pounding in my ears.

22

AT LAST THE END IS COMING CLEAR

"Heads up!" Trish screamed as I stepped onto the churned and scorched ground where the front of the senior home property used to be.

I stopped, my head snapping up to find her.

Trish was standing on the opposite side of the burnt field, not far from the Hellpit. She held up her hand, palm out, and nodded toward the face of the thing, which was bulging outward again.

On my side of the field, Bev was jogging toward me, looking tired and filthy.

An explosion of foul air ripped my attention back to the Hellmouth, and I watched in horror as several demons were blown out of it, sailing over the consecrated field and landing safely where the prayer chain had been before they were evacuated.

As the demons tucked and rolled, a foggy gray spell exploded above their heads, and Chief Marshal sprayed something into the mist the magic left behind.

The silvery mist rained down on the monsters and they exploded into dust upon contact.

"What's going on?" I asked Bev as she finally reached me.

She bent over, panting, and I noticed the blood and gore that coated her tee-shirt and stained her jeans in dark spots. "We had to adjust on the fly. Goddess-danged things somehow figured out about the consecrated ground, so they've been flying, riding, or being catapulted out to avoid it."

I frowned, wanting to ask her about the trustworthiness of her witches but realizing it wasn't the time. If we survived the night, we'd do a debrief and figure out what went wrong.

For the next time.

The thought made me shudder.

"What's with the mist?"

"It's Trish's trap." Bev grinned. "The spell is engaged when a demonic signature touches the ground beyond the sanctified area. We've been adding holy water to give it a wider range. The few demons who manage to avoid it are taken out by the royal lost."

My eyes went wide. "They showed up?"

"Yeah. They were late because they had to round up the demons who'd avoided us in town." Bev's eyes turned hard. "I'd like to know how they anticipated that trap. It was pure genius."

I'd like to know that myself. But I had a more pressing question for the moment. "Please tell me they didn't kill the possessed humans?"

Bev grinned. "No. They carried the hosts into the vortex and, when it spit them back out, the humans came out with them, leaving the demons behind."

"The Thomas's?" I asked hopefully. "Were their demons removed too?"

Her smile fell away. "They tried. The couple came back out of the Hellmouth the same. Their demons are apparently too tied into their souls for it to work."

My heart hurt for the young woman who'd tried to warn me about the homeless man that day, after the first demon attack. Tears blurred my vision. Sniffling, I nodded. "Okay. Thanks for letting me know."

An explosion rocked the area, literally knocking us to our knees from its power. Behind the Hellmouth, fire leaped into the sky, a sulfurous stench blowing over everyone.

Bev took a step in that direction. "Now what?" she asked, wearily scraping goo off her face. "I'm about done with these demons. We need to get this thing closed."

"It's the propane tank," I told her. "Something apparently ignited it."

I glanced that way and saw a small, stooped, and awkwardly-moving creature hurrying away from the scene. "Looks like a demon blew it up. I'll send Luke after it."

Bev nodded. "I need to get back. Are you going to be okay?" She nodded toward the Hellmouth.

"Sure. Yeah. No problem." I lifted my staff and tried to smile. But my lips wouldn't cooperate. "Hey, did you ever find Father Ignacious?"

She nodded, a grin tugging at her lips. "He was in his office. He's fine."

"Why was the church unlocked," I asked.

Bev let the grin go. "He was giving himself a facial and didn't want anyone to see him in his clay mask." She giggled.

"Goddess in a girdle," I said, shaking my head.

"Yeah," she agreed, her smile sliding away. She gave me an impulsive hug. I fought a grimace as the gore she was wearing transferred to me. When she pulled away, I almost flinched from the look in her eyes. “You will not throw your life away, Aggy. If cauterizing that thing from the outside doesn’t work, we’ll come up with another solution.”

My gaze wouldn’t quite meet hers, and she noticed. Grabbing my arms, she gave me a little shake. “Promise me.”

“Of course,” I said noncommittally. “Go. I’ll send Luke to get the demon and then smash Old Hellbreath into vapors.”

Her gaze searched mine for another beat, and then she nodded. “I love you, sis.” She turned and jogged slowly away.

Watching her lope back toward Mavis, I muttered, “I love you too.” Sighing, I sent a mental message to the wolf. *Luke, I need you to chase down the demon that just blew up the propane tank.*

He responded immediately. *I’m on it.*

As I neared the Hellmouth, sweat popped out all over my body. It wasn’t from nerves...well, not entirely...the thing was giving off a hellish level of heat. Combined with the putrid stench and the incessant screaming, it was enough to make a sane person run screaming from the place.

Apparently, I was insane.

“Madam Lares,” a familiar and very welcome voice called out behind me. “Are you ready?”

The smile I’d been struggling with a moment before miraculously appeared. “Princess! I’m glad you’re okay.”

She simply nodded, her stiff movements telling me she wasn’t a hundred percent yet. “We need to hurry. The warriors are amassing inside the vortex. Once they come out, it will be over.”

My smile died. “You mean it’s going to get worse?”

“Oh, yes. This...” She swept an arm over the battles raging all around us, “...is just a distraction. Hell’s armies are gathering beneath the surface. We have minutes if we're lucky. More likely seconds."

Taking a deep breath, I nodded. "Let's go."

"Before we go in there," the princess told me, her tone dire, "you must understand. Under no circumstances should you allow yourself to get separated from me. That's critical." She looked down at me, lines of worry creasing her brow. "If you're not with me when I'm thrown back out, you'll be left behind, and you will not be set free. An ancient warrior guardian is too fine a prize to release. Do you understand?"

Icy fear swelled in my chest. I had to fight to draw a breath. I opened my mouth to respond, but the complete horror inspired by her warning made it impossible for me to speak. Finally, I gave a quick jerk of my chin in agreement.

Without another word, Layla scooped me up, threw me over her shoulder, and took off running.

There are advantages to leading with your backend... literally. Bouncing along with a bony shoulder digging into my belly wasn't comfortable. And having my backside be the first thing anyone ahead of us saw was less than ideal, but there was the bonus of not knowing how close we'd gotten to the hated Hellmouth until it was too late to worry about it.

One moment I was sweating so much I thought I might slide right out of my clothes and onto the ground at Layla's feet, and the next, the world was a nausea-inducing whirl of bloody red energy mixed with blacker than black shadows and my entire body was on fire.

The screaming I'd heard from outside hit me like a rock-hewn fist, ripping any sense of composure away and reducing me to a quaking, shrieking mess.

Beneath my frantic, struggling form, Layla's body was like a collection of steel bands formed into its familiar shape. Her muscles strained as she seemed to force her way through the natural resistance the vortex generated.

I stopped screaming long enough to pull foul air into my lungs and then choked, coughing violently as the stench of brimstone and death coated my airways, making me retch.

My hair stuck to my soaking skin. My own stink rose up around me, making me grimace. The stench of fear and sweat and more fear had made me almost as repulsive as the Eau de demon that was the natural scent of the vortex.

Layla gave an energetic push, and the pressure around us finally broke. Like the popping of an eardrum returning hearing to normal, the overwhelming heat and the incessant caterwauling suddenly intensified. It was like walking out of the sunshine and into an apocalyptic wasteland.

At that moment, I experienced the full horror of the vortex.

Fire ate the landscape. Bodies were strewn throughout the space. Horrible, misshapen, tortured forms that crawled limped or dragged themselves forward toward a narrow red gash on the air that resembled the pupil in a snake's eye.

As I stared at it, the snake blinked, the edges of the gash undulating with fiery energy. It seemed to focus on us, widening as if realizing we were up to no good.

I would have screamed, except that Layla chose that moment to spin around. As she did, a harsh scraping of air grabbed hold of us and started to yank us backward toward that nightmare-inducing slit.

That was when I noticed the razor-like edges on the opening and realized it was going to slice us into pieces if we passed through it again.

Goddess in garters! We couldn't go out that way and survive.

My survival instincts made me spread my arms wide

looking for something to brace against, to keep from being sucked through the deadly snake's eye. With a breath-stealing whoosh, the sucking wind grabbed hold of me and ripped me out of Layla's grasp, flinging me toward the very thing I'd been trying to avoid.

23

THE GUARDIAN'S LOSS A THING TO FEAR

My screams reverberated through the vortex, returning to me in disconcerting waves that throbbed with such horror I couldn't believe the sound had come from me. But it *had* been me. My throat was raw from the endless screeching, and my chest hurt.

I hurdled helplessly toward the slicing edge of the gash, my mind shut down from terror.

Someone screamed my name from far away. One small corner of my brain registered the owner of the alarmed-sounding voice.

Before I could call out to Layla, a gruesome demon in the vortex's stream crashed into me, knocking me back a few feet and slamming me into something that seemed to consist of slime and razor-sharp snapping teeth.

I bounced away, the very air around me dense enough to hold me aloft. It was like floating in gelatin, yet the container had no sides or floor.

The demon I'd bumped into kept on moving through the stream leading it to the outside world.

To the earthly plane. To Rome. My people.

Remembering cleared my mind a little. My gaze locked onto the staff I still clutched in my hand. Resolve bloomed beneath the terror.

I remembered something else, too. Something that turned my bowels to ice.

If you're not with me when I'm flung out, you'll be left behind, and you will not escape. An ancient warrior guardian is too fine a prize to release. Do you understand?

Yes. I understood. I understood that I was lost.

Pulling myself upright, I looked around. I didn't see Layla anywhere in the swirling, disconcerting mess.

She was gone.

After a moment of panicked searching, I had to admit to myself that I'd been left behind. I scraped tears off my face and shoved the fear away, thinking of everyone I loved beyond the abyss. I couldn't save myself. But I could still save them.

Lifting my staff, I tugged at the magic in my core, pulling it forward.

An energetic roar sounded mere feet away, and I spun around, finding something the size of a small car barreling down on me. The thing was covered in reddish-brown fur, its face flat and its eyes small. The creature reminded me of a gorilla, except that it had a long tail. There were blade-like spines along the length of the demon's tail, and its hands and feet were like crab claws.

The creature reached out and snapped a claw near my face, its tail whipping toward me as I lifted my staff to ward it off.

Golden energy shot from the staff, spearing past the gorilla monster and exploding somewhere across the void. A screech of pain told me it had found a victim. But not the one I'd aimed for.

Agony sliced across my middle as the monster's tail carved into the flesh at my waist. The spines sliced deep, like tiny spears that burned with fire wherever they touched.

I screamed, my already sore throat scraped to the bleeding point as I slammed the staff into the monster's head, trying to keep it from sinking its teeth into me too.

My blows barely fazed the thing. The gorilla monster snapped at the staff with its jaws, but I managed to keep the weapon away from its teeth, only to have it clasped in one of the large pincers that served as its hands.

The first yank nearly pulled the staff out of my grip. I couldn't allow a second tug. If I lost my weapon, I wouldn't live very long in that inhospitable place.

Reaching into my core, I jerked as much magic as I could forward, feeding it into my staff.

The energy blasted out of the orb and pierced the monster's ugly face, ripping a fist-sized hole in its forehead and blazing deeper into the vortex. In the distance, a wave of fire flared up, the flames taking their share of carnage with them if the screaming I heard was any indication.

I shoved free of the gorilla monster and watched it slide on down the stream. My forward momentum stopped. I hung motionless and looked around. That was when I realized the demon had carried me much closer to the snake's eye before I'd gotten free of it. I spun around and felt my eyes go wide as the gleaming blades of the gash slammed closed behind the corpse of the gorilla monster.

I was twenty feet away from that opening. Thirty at the most. Distance was hard to discern in the swirling, discombobulating abyss.

I watched the blades carefully, trying to discern a pattern. Maybe I could find an opportunity to slip through.

The gelatinous atmosphere shuddered and stilled. A

distant drone, like the sound of thousands of boots pounding against the ground, brought my head up and my gaze to the swirling chaos behind me. I squinted at what appeared to be a heavy, dark line in the distance, its form irregular and strangely man-shaped. With a jolt, I realized what it was.

Hell's army was on the march.

I looked from the marching army to the snake's eye and knew I had no choice. I'd rather die the quick death in front of me than let the enemy behind take me prisoner.

I had to get to that gash.

I tried to move forward but the jelly held me in place. For a moment, I hung there, my gaze sliding around at the creatures in the vortex with me. Unlike me, they were still moving forward.

Then, with a jolt, I was moving again, but I was going the wrong way!

The jelly-like atmosphere seemed to come alive with another spasm. A low moan fed through the stuff, throbbing against my skin. I concentrated on the change, trying to read it.

It felt like...rage.

The jelly juddered again, the action much more violent than before, and I was tossed sideways. I lost my balance and my sense of direction was ripped away as I tumbled through the jelly.

The vortex shuddered again, like a small explosion, and a roar erupted all around me. The sound sent the gelatinous atmosphere into motion, the waves of jelly churning the space where I hung until I felt as if I were riding an inflatable giraffe over a deadly rapids.

I was thrown this way and that, then spun around and rolled head over heels. I could barely feel my body anymore in the chaos of movement, let alone form a plan to escape it.

"Madam Lares?" The voice was buried beneath the maelstrom of motion and the soft roar that worked its way continually through the vortex. I tried to lift my head to find the owner but couldn't see anything beyond the flailing of my own body.

"Madam..." The voice was slightly louder that time, but it was cut off in the middle as if its owner was battling the same chaotic environment I was trying to navigate.

Beneath it all, there was a rhythmic snap, snap, snapping sound that I fought to identify.

"Aggy!" The voice exploded behind me, its owner so close I could probably reach out and...

Something grabbed my wrist, yanking me in.

I yelped and instinctively tried to escape the grip.

A fist glanced off my temple. "Stop fighting me. I'm trying to save your life," Layla growled out.

I went limp and let relief wash over me.

The chaos flung me around like a loose rope in a windstorm until Layla managed to grab me around the waist and drag me up against her much bigger body. There, with my frame enveloped in hers, the maelstrom softened.

The drone of marching boots was closer. In my panic, I thought it sounded faster too. "Hurry! I told Layla. They're coming."

"I'm aware," she screamed back, fighting to keep us on a direct stream toward the snake's eye ahead.

Snap.

Snap.

Snap.

I looked up into Layla's face, but she wasn't looking at me. "What is that...?"

"Get ready to do what you need to do!" she interrupted, all but yelling into my face.

I shook off my curiosity. Whatever that snapping noise was, there was nothing I could do about it. But I could, hopefully, do something about the goddess-be-damned vortex.

Snap.

Snap.

Sna...

We shot through the gash, the sharp edges scraping across my arm as I lifted my staff.

SNAP!

I felt Layla's body jolt and then she yelled, "Now!"

Sending energy into the staff, I bore down on it, expelling a dense wave of golden energy between the bladed edges of the vortex gash. I screamed from the effort as I forced the magic past the entrance and as deeply into the abyss as I could make it go.

The gash shuddered, flickered, and then went still, the edges easing closed with a final snap.

I watched in disappointment as the thing just sat there, a mockery of everything we'd gone through trying to kill it from the inside out.

We shot away from the entrance, still caught in the stream. Tears slid down my cheeks as we hit the outside barrier and shoved it outward, Layla clawing frantically to slice it open so it would spit us out.

I hung in her grip, my heart breaking as I stared at the closed snake eye. Its very wholeness seemed to mock me.

"Aggy!" Layla screamed. "Help me, or we're going to go up with the vortex!"

I shook my head. "It's not..."

A deep rumble, like the growl of a massive dragon, came from everywhere at once.

"Hurry!" she screamed in my face.

The rumble grew and the vortex trembled beneath it, spears of light shooting through in first one spot and then another. Each beam was like acid against the putrid evil in that shadowed place, burning, disinfecting.

With a jolt of understanding, I realized. "That's sunlight."

The vortex started to shake from side to side. We were flung away from the exterior membrane, and Layla screamed again. "Aggy, do it now!"

I reached around with my staff and sent energy into the membrane, giving it everything I had left. Which turned out to be not all that much. My body was depleted, worn out, and weak.

But I needn't have worried. My magic ripped through the weakened membrane like a hot blade through soft butter.

As soon as I opened a hole to the outside world, an unseen force grabbed us and yanked us through it. We slammed to the ground and skidded several feet, my lungs devoid of air and every bone in my body aching as we slid to a stop.

"Get them out of there!" someone screamed. "Hurry!"

I lay limply on the ground, a painful light burning through my eyelids. Heat bathed my body and I welcomed it, smiling as the comforting warmth eased some of the achiness from my bones and muscles.

There was a wave of frantic activity around us. Hands grabbed hold and tugged me gently out of Layla's grip.

I heard a sharp exclamation of pain and wondered who was hurt. But then gentle hands scooped me up and the world went bumpy as the person holding me started to run. I recognized the scent and smiled, snuggling up against a broad chest. “Gren.”

A soft touch of lips against my forehead. “You’re okay, beautiful Aggy. I’ve got you now.”

I sighed, just as another explosion sent everything flying, and the concussion blasted my protector and me into the air, the stench of sulfurous smoke mixing with the sting of debris crashing all around us.

My world went blessedly dark.

24

WHEN GOLDEN DAYS RETURN AT LAST

Birds sang a pretty song outside my window. A ray of sunshine bathed my left arm and the place where I lay felt wonderfully soft. The sweet scent of flowers wafted over me on a gentle breeze.

A soft sigh preceded the shifting of a small body next to my thigh. I opened my eyes to discover I was in my own bed, the construction mess I'd grown accustomed to still cluttering one end of the room, and the sun beyond my open window low enough to tease the tops of the distant tree line.

I slid my hand over Monty's sleek head and he licked his lips, snuggling closer to my leg with another sigh.

My smile widened. It was good to be home. And alive.

The memory of my visit to the inside of the devilish Hellmouth invaded my thoughts and put a strain on my happiness. I tried to shove it away, but it was too late. The happy-stupid sensation I'd awoken with was gone.

I sat up and carefully shifted my legs out from under my little hero.

A soft chirp made me stop and glance up.

The bat was hanging from my light fixture, its yellow

eyes open and focused on me. "Bathilda. How's it hangin'?" I chuckled at my own joke. "Get it? You're a bat. You're hanging."

The creature stared at me as if I were beyond stupid. It could be right.

"Hey, we all deal with stress in different ways," I told the bat. I headed into the bathroom and took care of business, then pulled on a pair of yoga pants and a tee-shirt and shuffled down the hall toward the kitchen.

I'd only taken a few steps before I heard the soft thump of Monty's oversized doxie feet hitting the floor. He came through the bedroom door and ran to me, eyes bright and tail wagging. "You hungry, sweet boy?"

He bounced around my feet a few times and then zoomed into the kitchen, rounded the table, and zoomed back my way.

I laughed. "Okay, give me a minute. I'm moving slow today." As soon as I said the words, I realized it was true. My middle-aged body had taken quite a few hits the day before... I stopped in the middle of that thought. Had it been the day before? I had no idea. It could have been a few hours earlier, for all I knew. Or a week.

I filled Monty's bowl before starting my coffee. Never let it be said that I didn't have my priorities in order. Then I dug around in the refrigerator while the coffee brewed. By the time black, hot coffee steamed from my mug, I had a bagel in the toaster and was starting to wake up.

I looked around for my cell phone, thinking about who I should call to find out what happened after Layla and I went into the vortex. I couldn't call Niele or Gren or Ferral because they didn't have phones that I knew of. I frowned. I needed to fix that.

I could just give them a mental shout like I usually did.

But, it didn't seem right to bark a command at them for non-emergency things.

I stood there dithering. Was it an emergency? My council's welfare was a key component of my job...my life. I cared about them all. Even...gulp...Ferral. He drove me crazy, but he was growing on me. Slowly. Very slowly. With exquisite slowness.

I shook the thought away. I wanted to see Gren. I wanted to know if he was okay. The memory of that explosion and the way it had sent us flying had my heart palpitating in my chest.

I really wanted to call my mom or sister. So, that was what I did. Mavis answered on the second ring. "I know! I'm sorry. I forgot the cream cheese, and Bev was supposed to be there an hour ago, but she had car trouble. Ferral's going to kill me for leaving you alone..."

"Mom!" I interrupted. "I'm fine. I didn't call to give you a hard time. I just wanted to make sure you were okay. And Bev. And everybody."

Her sigh sifted through the line. "Everybody's fine, honey. There's a lot to tell you. I'll be there in ten minutes, okay?"

"That's fine. Don't rush. I'm just relieved to hear your voice."

"Me too, honey. I was..." She sniffed, and I could visualize her shaking her head to expel whatever emotion was weighing her down. "I'll be there soon. And don't feed that brat of a dog. He's already conned your sister and me into feeding him this afternoon. I think he's eaten five or six times today with everybody coming and going."

I laughed, giving Monty a look. He grinned up at me, not looking the least bit contrite. "Make that six or seven. I'll see you soon." I hung up and fixed my bagel, settling for butter and jelly since I was apparently out of cream cheese.

A few minutes later, Mavis blew into my home carrying bags of groceries. She dropped them on the table, wrapping me in a hug without saying a word. I hugged her back so tight I made her squeak. Loosening my grip, I apologized.

She scraped the back of her hand under her eyes and sniffled. "No worries, honey." Giving me a smile, she patted my cheek. "You look good. Any aches or pains?"

I laughed. "Only my whole body. I'm too old for this stuff."

"You're not even close to old, honey." Mavis grabbed for the bags, but I got to them first.

"I'll put them away," I told her. "You sit."

It was an indication of how hard the battle had been on her that she took me up on the offer. "Thanks. I am a little tired. We used a lot of magic out there."

I made quick work of the groceries and returned to the table with a bakery box. I didn't know what was in it, but it smelled like vanilla and sugar. Whatever it was, it was going into my mouth. I was suddenly starving.

I made Mavis coffee and sat back down with her. "Tell me what happened after Layla and I went into the vortex."

She shook her head. "Girl, you are going to be the death of me."

"I came back out, just like I promised." There was no need to tell her I'd been pretty sure for a while there that I wasn't coming back. What she didn't know couldn't hurt her.

"*Two* days later!"

My mug stopped halfway to my mouth. I blinked at her, certain I hadn't heard right. "Two days?"

She nodded, flipping the box open and extracting a massive chocolate chip cookie from it. "Longest two days of my life."

"Oh, mom. I'm so sorry."

She shook her head, but her mouth was full, so she didn't respond. I sat there, stunned for a long moment, then realized what that meant. "You were all out there battling demons for two days?"

"Yes and no. Thank the goddess for Layla's people. They did most of the fighting. By the end, I was relegated to making sure everybody had coffee, water, and donuts." She puffed out her cheeks. "Danny's donuts in Huberville was the only place I could find open in the area. Nothing was open in Rome, and I didn't want to drive the hour to Indianapolis." She winced. "I never want to see another donut as long as I live."

I eyed the cookie she was snarfing. "Cookies are much better anyway."

Totally missing my sarcasm, Mavis nodded. "Right?"

I grabbed a cookie too. The first bite nearly made me swoon. "Oh my goddess! This is the best thing I've ever tasted."

Mavis grinned. "We have a new bakery in town. I'll take you by there soon and introduce you to Tilly. She's a sweetheart and a magician with flour, sugar, and butter."

"I can't disagree with that." Taking another bite, I chewed and swallowed, broaching the subject I was most worried about. "The townspeople who were possessed?"

Mavis's smile slid away and she sighed. "The lost ones de-possessed most of them by doing what Layla did with you. They're all fine. Except..." She put the cookie down as if she'd suddenly lost her appetite.

"Who didn't make it?" I asked, already feeling their loss before I had a name or a face.

"That poor young couple."

"They died?" I asked, shoving my own cookie away.

"No. But they won't wake up." She forced a smile. "The good news is that the changes made to their bodies stopped once the Hellmouth died." She grimaced. "They didn't get any worse."

"But they didn't improve either," I guessed.

She shook her head. "No."

"What about Shadee?"

Mavis swallowed cookie. "She's doing really well. Her coven has been bathing her in healing spells. Her hair is even starting to grow back." Mavis patted my hand. "She wants to see you...to explain how she ended up above that Hellpit."

"I'll go see her tomorrow. Can you give me the high points?"

"She was trying to slow it down and it grabbed her. It really wasn't her fault, Aggy." She gave me puppy-dog eyes and I nodded. "I'm not blaming her."

We sat in silence for a moment.

"What happened inside that thing?" Mavis finally asked in a small voice.

I thought about her question for a beat and then shook my head. "If you don't mind, I'd rather not talk about that yet. I need some time to make sense of it in my brain."

Mavis gave my hand a squeeze. "Of course, honey."

"Tell me about when Layla and I came out. I remember a lot of yelling and then an explosion." My eyes went wide. "What about the senior home? Is there anything left of the building?"

"Nothing but charred earth. But they can rebuild."

I grimaced. “Over a Hellmouth? Maybe not the best idea.”

She shrugged. “They still own the land.”

“How’s Layla?”

“The princess was…hurt when you came out.”

“Is she okay?”

Mavis refused to look me in the eye, but her voice was determinedly cheerful when she responded. “She’ll be just fine. She’s with a healer right now.”

“That’s good,” I said, but I watched her carefully. Something about her response seemed suspicious. “What was going on when we flew out of there?”

“Well, we knew you were close because the healthy demons that had been spewing out of that thing for hours were suddenly coming out mangled or dead.” She gave a violent shudder. “That thing that looked like a demonic King Kong…” She shuddered again. “Horrible.”

That reminded me of the spiky tail, and I surreptitiously felt around my waist, finding tenderness but no pain. Somebody must have healed me. Magic had some truly wonderful benefits. “I actually had a run-in with that guy. I’m pretty sure he’ll star in my nightmares for a while.”

“Ugh!” Mavis said. “Then we saw Layla clawing at the membrane, and we knew you were trying to get out. We had our heads together trying to figure out if we could open it with a spell when you blasted a hole in it and came flying out. You hit the ground so hard we were sure you must have broken every bone in your bodies.”

“Did we?” I asked softly.

She shook her head but didn’t elaborate.

“And the explosion?”

She widened her eyes at me. “That Hellmouth was wobblin’ and shakin’ and making these horrible growling sounds. When the ground bubbled up around it, we knew something was going to blow soon."

"The ground bubbled?"

"Yes! It was like standing on the ocean during a hurricane. We grabbed you up and got you out of there as soon as we could, but you still got dinged by the front edge of the blast. If Gren hadn't leaped into the air and flown you away, you probably would have gotten sucked up in the backwash."

"Backwash?"

She nodded enthusiastically. "Anything demonic on our side of the vortex, dead or alive, got pulled back into the abyss just before it disappeared."

I thought of the pretty white horse, a sadness filling my chest.

The front door slammed. "Hello?" a familiar voice called out.

"In the kitchen," I yelled.

Wanda stomped heavily down the hallway and stopped at the door as my dog attacked her with kisses and a manically wagging tail. She bent down and scratched his ears. "Hey, dude. How's things?"

I grinned at how at home she seemed. When had that happened?

Wanda's gaze lifted to mine, and I saw the worry there. "Aggy." She straightened, twining her fingers and shifting uncomfortably on her feet. "I'm glad you're home."

I stood up and walked over, wrapping her in a hug.

She stiffened with alarm, her arms down at her sides, and then her muscles softened, and she wrapped her skinny arms around me, holding me tight. "I was worried."

"I know, honey. I'm sorry."

She took a long breath that hitched slightly in the

middle and squeezed me tighter.

When the front door opened again, several voices finding their way to us, Wanda stepped away, giving me a shy smile. “You go ahead and visit,” she said, moving toward the cupboards. “I’ll feed Monty for you.”

“No!” Mavis and I said together.

25

THE LARES MUST LOOK TO THE PAST

Happy chaos ensued over the next few hours. Everyone except Gren, Ferral, and the two bird members of my crew arrived to check on me and then stayed to visit. Niele wore the new mossy shorts Bev had made him, transforming him from being a man in a diaper to one in shorts. The chest, legs, and feet were still bare, but...baby steps.

Wanda stayed until well into the night before she went upstairs to visit with Bathilda before she was pulled away.

Monty managed to eat his weight in treats and people food. He was definitely losing his waistline. I'd need to either put him on a diet or start him...and me...on a more strenuous exercise regime.

After exchanging stories about the battle from each person's viewpoint, we'd eaten a delicious meal of pasta primavera, made with home-grown vegetables and washed down with liberal amounts of a very good red wine. Trish had cooked the dinner, with Luke as her kitchen slave and Wanda as the official dish washer.

We'd talked and debriefed and celebrated the return to normal until I started yawning, and everyone left so I could go to bed.

Unfortunately, after they left I was too keyed up to sleep. And I was worried about Gren.

"Madam Lares."

I jerked in surprise at the sound of Ferral's voice. He walked out of the night and joined me on my patio. He didn't sit. Instead, he stood at the edge of the patio with his hands clasped before him, looking very serious.

"You missed a delicious dinner tonight."

He nodded. "Yes. I had odds and ends to clean up."

I could only imagine how many odds and ends there were. Starting the next day, I was going to do some of that myself. I planned to visit everyone in Rome over the next few days and make sure they were all okay.

"You're looking fit," Ferral said.

"Thanks, advocate. I'm feeling better."

He nodded. "You did well."

I nearly fell off my chair. The words of praise sounded as though they were wrenched from his throat with a giant pair of pliers, but they were still nice to hear. "Um. Thanks." I lifted my glass. "Would you like some wine?"

"No. But thank you. I can't stay. I only came to give you a report on the woman."

I frowned. "The woman?"

He nodded. "Yes. The one who was possessed by the demon."

"Ah. Yes. Mavis already told me. Have she and her husband woken up?"

His blond brows lowered with confusion. "I'm referring to the elderly woman. Mrs. Wolde."

"Oh." Then my mind recalled his words. "She was possessed?"

"Yes. She is the answer to the mystery of how the demons gained advance knowledge of our battle strategies."

The realization plunked into place in my mind. "Of course. She was in the kitchen while we were discussing our plans."

Ferral nodded.

I thought back, remembering the bent, lumbering gait I'd mistaken for a demon in the dark. It could just as easily have been an elderly woman moving through the darkness. "She blew up the propane tank." I covered my mouth in horror. Poor Mrs. Wolde. "Is she all right?"

He nodded again. "Physically, yes. Unfortunately, it appears she was responsible for calling that shadow demon that nearly killed you and the princess. And she is likely the one who opened the vortex. We've learned from speaking to the nurse, Shadee, that Mrs. Wolde was a dark witch in her youth. Her family believed she'd put all that behind her. Clearly, they were wrong."

I shook my head. "What will we do with her?"

"She is with Princess Layla's people. They have the means to imprison a dark witch and make sure she doesn't escape again."

"What about Molly Stanton? Has anybody found her?"

"She turned up back at the hospital, only slightly the worse for wear." He frowned at me. "I know you were friends with Molly…"

Something in his gaze warned me he had bad news. "She's possessed isn't she?"

"We believe she *was* possessed. The demon seems to have moved on. But her soul is stained. She can't be allowed around non-magical humans anymore. She has magic and might use it to harm people."

"What does that mean? Where will she go?"

Ferral stared at his clasped hands, clearly thinking something he didn't want to share with me.

"What?" I asked.

He slid me a sideways glance. "We've come up with a solution, of sorts. It's not perfect, but your friend would be made safe and comfortable."

I raised my brows, waiting for him to go on.

"Princess Layla has offered to keep her with them. She can create a...comfortable space for Molly to live out her years."

"You mean a prison."

He extended his hands, palms up.

I didn't like it. Not one bit. I had a feeling that, once Molly was with the lost ones, we'd never see her again. "I need to think on that. We can't give up on trying to save her."

Ferral gave me a small bow. "Of course. For the moment, she is safely contained. Have a restful night, Madam Lares."

After he left, I rested my head against the back of my chair and let the weariness take me over. I might have dozed off because my first awareness that I wasn't alone was when Monty bumped my leg as he surged to his feet and started barking.

I sat upright, energy spitting from my fingertips as the night split apart just beyond the arc of the patio light.

The tall, familiar form that strode toward me through the muted light eased my fear. I allowed the magic to recede and smiled at Gren as he approached. "I was wondering where you'd gone."

His apologetic glance eased the last of the tension from my chest. "I do apologize, beautiful Aggy." Gren crouched down to scratch my furry little protector behind his floppy ears. "I had an important task to complete before coming."

"Oh?"

He straightened. "I paid a visit to Princess Layla."

"Is she all right?" I tensed, fearing she'd taken a turn for the worse.

"She is..." He slid his hands into the pockets of his jeans. I took a moment to admire the fit of those jeans before returning my attention to his words. "...physically well. But the experience has changed her."

That didn't sound good. "How can I help?"

Running long fingers through his mahogany hair, Gren sat down next to me. "At the moment, there is nothing anyone can do. She must adjust to her new reality. When she is ready, she will come to you."

Curiosity buried its claws into me and held on. "That sounds dire. Tell me what's going on."

"I do not wish to disappoint you," he said, his tone filled with tension. "But I made a vow..."

"I just want to help."

He inclined his head. "The princess has requested that I not share her predicament. It will please her if you honor that request."

Our gazes held for a long moment. I finally broke the stalemate with a sigh. "Okay. But I owe her my life twice-over," I reminded him. "If she's in trouble, I need to know so I can help."

"She is not in trouble. She's just coming to terms with some things."

I nodded.

We fell silent, listening to the night sounds around us. The song of the crickets. The occasional hooting of an owl high in the trees. The distant chorus of the coyotes. The sounds calmed me deep down in my soul. For the first time since defeating the vortex, I felt the real world fold around me again, comforting in its normalcy.

From the place where he slept beneath the table, Monty's head snapped up, his bright brown gaze locked on something in the graveyard.

Before I could grab hold of his collar, he was off, running toward the mix of ancient and contemporary stones highlighted by the silver glow of the full moon overhead.

I was on my feet, hurrying after him before I gave it much thought.

A silvered shadow moved among the stones and, atop her usual gravestone, Wraith waited with a snapping tail for her friend to arrive.

Father Dodson lifted an insubstantial hand to me, and I returned the wave. He was wispier than usual, probably depleted from the massive task of consecrating the entire town of Rome.

Gren appeared next to me, linking his arm with mine. "It appears things are back to normal, Madam Lares."

I arched a brow at him. "You're supposed to call me Aggy when we're off duty, remember?"

He lifted my arm and placed a lingering kiss over the pulse point on my wrist. "I do. But I sometimes feel the need to remind you how special you are."

That brought a frown to my face. "I'm special because I'm the Lares?"

"Of course." His warm lips found the inside of my other wrist, serving up a tender touch there that made me shiver with delight. "And in so many ways."

My body arched toward his, suddenly unable to sustain the distance between us.

His lips curved upward. "You astound me with your talents. You achieved the impossible, defeating a Hellmouth and coming out of it alive." His lips found my temple, lingered there. "And, it seems you have mastered the use of your staff at last."

I snorted out a laugh. "Mastered? Not even close. But I'm reasonably certain I can use it without blowing off my own nose at least."

Gren lowered his head, pressing a tender kiss to the tip of my nose. "I am relieved to hear it." Then he was stepping back, releasing my hands. "I'll let you rest. I'm sure there will be much to do tomorrow." He gave me a slight bow, the action making him seem like a prince from a far different time. "Goodnight, sweet Aggy."

"Night, Gren." I watched him until the shadows swallowed him up and then called to Monty and started back to the house.

Movement high above my head drew my gaze to the belfry, and a pale face that was lifted toward the moon above. Wanda looked sad and thoughtful, and I got the sense it was an expression she hid from everyone else.

It was odd to see her there so late at night.

She was no doubt lonely, and she certainly missed her mom. I'd been so wrapped up in my own problems, I hadn't done anything to help her get her life back.

Even as my mind formed the thought, her pale form began to fade away, until I wondered if I'd imagined seeing her there. Bothered by the vision of her pensive expression and feeling guilty for letting life distract me from helping her, I made myself a promise.

I was moving her problem to the top of my To-Do list.

We were going to figure out how to remove that witches' hex on the teen. I owed her that. And, more importantly, I *wanted* to help. She hadn't had a lot of people in her life she could count on.

I wanted her to consider me one of the few.

The End

DON'T MISS OUT

Stay up on all Sam's news by joining her newsletter, and get a copy of a fun mystery just for signing up!

SIGN UP HERE!
https://samcheever.com/newsletter/

ABOUT THE AUTHOR

USA Today and Wall Street Journal Bestselling Author Sam Cheever writes mystery and suspense, creating stories that draw you in and keep you eagerly turning pages. Known for writing great characters, snappy dialogue, and unique and exhilarating stories, Sam is the award-winning author of 100+ books.

To learn more about Sam and her work, visit her at one of her online hotspots:

www.samcheever.com

samcheever@samcheever.com

ALSO BY SAM CHEEVER

If you enjoyed **What Voodoo Do You Do That?**, you might also enjoy these other fun series by Sam. To find out more, visit the **BOOKS** page at www.samcheever.com:

Mature Magic Paranormal Women's Fiction

(for more fun adventures with Aggy and Monty!)

Enchanting Inquiries Paranormal Cozy Mysteries

Yesterday's Paranormal Mysteries

Reluctant Familiar Paranormal Mysteries

Country Cousin Mysteries

Silver Hills Cozy Mysteries

Gainfully Employed Mysteries

Honeybun Heat Series

www.ingramcontent.com/pod-product-compliance
Lightning Source LLC
LaVergne TN
LVHW010055110826
845155LV00028B/343

* 9 7 8 1 9 5 0 3 3 1 7 9 6 *